That Old Cape Cod
By
Erni Johnson

Dedication

To Ric, for creating our Saturday Writer's Workshop,
in which this novel began and grew.

And, as always, to Daryl, who is as much a part
of my "old Cape Cod" as he is of me.

This a book of fiction and while many of the settings are modeled after actual Cape Cod locations, the characters and events of the plot are not real, but merely products of the author's imagination. I would, however, like to thank the owners of Pilgrim Village in Chatham, for allowing me to explore the memories of my youth, while walking the paths of their property one late fall afternoon. And also, for permitting me to photograph those scenic environs for the cover of this book, as well as the inspiration for the novel's peaceful and sentimental setting.

"If you're fond of sand dunes and salty air
Quaint little villages here and there
You're sure to fall in love with old Cape Cod,
Cape Cod, that old Cape Cod.
If you like the taste of a lobster stew,
Served by a window with an ocean view,
You're sure to fall in love with old Cape Cod.
Winding roads that seem to beckon you,
Miles of green beneath a sky of blue,
Church bells chiming on a Sunday morn,
Remind you of the town where you were born.
If you spend an evening you'll want to stay.
Watching the moonlight on Cape Cod Bay,
You're sure to fall in love with that old Cape Cod."

From "Old Cape Cod" sung by Patti Page (1957)
Music by Milton Yakus and Allan Jeffrey
Based on a poem written by Claire Rothrock

Chapter One: Emma (2003)

"What is this, some sort of midlife crisis?" Emma's brother, Stephen demanded when she called him that afternoon and laid out her plan.

"Of course not," Emma replied calmly, cradling the phone between her ear and shoulder, as she continued watering the plants on the window sill. "How can I be having a midlife crisis when I'm not even 40 years-old?"

Stephen ignored the logic.

"I'm pretty sure when Dad left us this money, he intended for us to use it for something practical," he declared, adding, "our parents were very practical people, as you recall."

"Ah," Emma responded, "the practical brother speaks...like you would know something about this trait."

"I'm very practical," Stephen said. "When was I not practical?"

"How much time do you have?" Emma asked.

There was a brief silence on the other end of the line.

"Okay," Stephen said finally. "But did you at least look around and see what else is available for the same money?"

Emma sighed.

"I don't want something else," she said. "In fact, I don't even know if I want to run this kind of business in the first place. But if I'm going to own a cottage colony, it has to be on Cape Cod, and it has to be this one."

"Well," Stephen replied reluctantly, "at least I can give you some furniture for the place. It ought to fit right into your vintage establishment."

"Very funny," Emma said. Stephen and his partner, Jim, owned an antique business and had just used her brother's recent inheritance to expand into a second storefront in the next town. Talk about impractical, Emma thought; two whole stores full of dusty, musty couches and chairs that threatened to break every time you sat on them...not to mention what was stored in the rented warehouse nearby. It was like visiting the remains of endless strangers' lives every time she entered one of these places. In fact, it wouldn't particularly surprise her to see an occasional ghost sitting on one of the faded Victorian sofas.

Of course, Emma was not really convinced that practicality got you much of anywhere in this world anyhow. After all, she now taught English in the same small private school she'd attended herself in Albany, New York, and her rented house was less than two blocks away from the one in which she grew up. Added to this was the fact that she had not even bought her own furniture, preferring instead to eat her morning cereal at the same yellow Formica table where she'd aimlessly stirred the Cheerios of her youth. Even her clothes were now stuffed in the heavy oak bureau she'd first acquired in childhood, which was far too big for the bedroom in which she now slept.

"How's my favorite nephew?" Stephen inquired, adroitly changing the subject as usual, Emma observed.

"You mean, your only nephew?" she teased. Emma's other brother, Joel, with all his macho swaggering and house full of sports memorabilia had managed to only produce female offspring.

"Yeah," Stephen said, "that one."

"Fifteen," Emma replied.

"What?"

"Luke's fifteen," she repeated, "that should give you a pretty good sense of how he is."

"Joel fifteen or Stephen fifteen?" her brother asked.

"Somewhere in between," Emma said. "How about my favorite brother-in-law?"

"Of which you also only have one," Stephen said. "Jim's fine, and by the way, we both know that you like him best."

"I absolutely do," she answered and laughed.

"Okay then," Stephen announced, "how about you call him to come and help you fix up that so-called resort when you buy it?"

"Maybe I just will," Emma said, and hung up.

Although her father's death had been a sudden shock to Emma, it seemed to her as though her brothers more or less took the whole thing in stride, which made her wonder, once again, if they had always known more about her parents than she did.

Joel, for example, had just shrugged sadly at the news and then remarked, "well, I guess we should have seen it coming...after all, with his heart the way it was, it was only a matter of time."

"What do you mean, with his heart the way it was?" Emma demanded. "Just last week he was out working in the garden!"

"My point exactly," Joel replied. "Something a man in his condition should not have been doing."

"There's no way you could have known, Emma," Stephen told her later. "Dad never talked to you about it, because he didn't want you to worry."

"He always felt like you had enough on your plate without stressing about him," her brother added.

But Emma was furious with both of them. They'd done the same thing to her when she was away at college, and her mother was diagnosed with cancer. It wasn't until the summer after she graduated that her father finally told her "Mom's been sick." And then, of course, it was too late to do much more than just come home and sit by her mother's bedside for those last few weeks.

Not that she could have done anything even if she knew, as Stephen pointed out over and over again that summer. But still, the whole thing was completely unfair. Maybe if she'd just married David instead of deciding to raise Luke on her own...what was it David said to her when she told him she was pregnant? "I guess I could marry you if that's what you want?" Or something like that. Of course, she'd turned him down. But then telling him she was getting an abortion and immediately breaking up with him when he just sort of shrugged and said, "Whatever you say." Okay, that was the right thing to do as well, except that it left Luke with no chance of ever knowing who his father was. Not that Luke ever seemed too interested, which was kind of odd in itself, Emma thought.

Maybe it would have been a better decision if she'd taken her father up on his offer to work for him, instead of waiting tables while she struggled to get her teaching degree. Or perhaps be like Joel, who

4

told their parents he had this high paying job, when in truth, he was making more money gambling on the weekends than in his so-called "professional position." Even Stephen, whose successful antique business Emma's father raved about to all his friends, never mentioned to his parents that his "partner" was also that in a different sense as well. At least she was honest about her life, such as it was.

Ah well, water under the bridge as they say, Emma mused, as she sat down at the kitchen table and sifted through the day's mail. As usual, there wasn't much of interest...a few seed catalogues leftover from the year Emma decided to grow her own vegetables (but somehow never quite got around to it), the electric bill (which seemed to grow more each year than anything she'd ever planted), and a few random envelopes addressed to Emma Lakin or Current Resident. Can't wait to read the exciting contents of those, she thought.

"An exercise in futility," was what her father would have called the way in which Emma scrutinized the daily contents of her mailbox, but even after all these years she just couldn't help it. Ever since she and her friend, Skip, had promised to be "pen pals" when they were just ten years-old, she could never get past that faint feeling of anticipation every time she walked down the driveway to get the mail. She only heard from him occasionally these days, but even then, she never told her brothers about the infrequent communication. It was enough that they'd teased her mercilessly about "her little boyfriend" back when they were kids, but now that they were adults, she suspected it would be even worse. For once she would have her own secrets, she decided.

"Who's this guy?" Luke had asked her earlier that day when he found some old pictures in the back of a drawer. The color photo he held in his hand was cracked and faded, but when Emma peered at it closely, she could see a little girl and a little boy, their arms around each other's shoulders, leaning against a scrub pine in front of a small white cottage.

"Oh," she said, "that's me and my friend, Skip. Haven't seen that picture for a while. Where did you find it?"

"In my desk drawer," Luke said. "Kind of stuck in the back."

"Huh," Emma remarked as she went back to drying the bowl in her hand and set it on the counter. "I guess that's because your desk used to be my desk when I was a kid, and I must have left some stuff in there."

Luke took the picture over to the window and holding it up to the light, studied it carefully.

"Where are you in this picture?" he asked. "It doesn't look like Gramps's house."

"It's a place we used to go in the summer," Emma told him, "on Cape Cod. That's where Skip and I met."

"Cape Cod?" Luke asked.

"Yeah," Emma replied. "It's in Massachusetts, out by the ocean."

"I don't see the ocean in this picture," Luke said, as he held the photo closer.

"No, you wouldn't," Emma said. "Cape Cod is on the ocean, but the cottage, well, it was on the water, but where there was a lot less water."

"Like a lake?" Luke asked.

"Sort of," Emma said.

"Huh," her son replied, then laid the picture on the table. "What happened to him?"

"Who?" Emma said, as she went back to drying the dishes in the drainboard.

"The guy in the picture," Luke said. "Your friend you met on Cape Cod. And how come I never met him?"

"Actually, you did meet him once," Emma said. She turned and picked up the photograph and examined it thoughtfully. Even though the picture was old and worn, Emma could still tell that the path on which the two children stood was thick with pine needles no one saw the necessity to remove, and that the cottage behind them, though possibly in need of a coat of paint, was still warm and welcoming.

"I did?" Luke said, peering over his mother's shoulder for a closer look at the photo. "When?"

"It was that time we went to Florida with Gramps," Emma explained, as she set the picture back on the kitchen table. "You were a little kid...maybe five or six?"

"Oh yeah," Luke said. "When Gramps took us to Disney World, right? And I went on Space Mountain with Uncle Stephen and I threw up?"

"That's the time," Emma said. What an endearing memory, she thought. Thank God "Gramps" wasn't here to share that lovely reminiscence.

"We also went to visit a friend of Uncle Stephen's in Fort Pierce and that's where you met Skip," she added. "I took you to the beach while your uncle hung out with his friend and that's where we saw him."

"He helped you build a sandcastle," Emma offered helpfully. Luke eyed her dubiously.

"It was kind of weird actually," she went on. "I mean I knew he lived there and everything, but it had been a while since we'd seen each

7

other, and I wasn't sure if I should even try and look him up. But then there we were, down on the beach and suddenly there he was walking toward us!"

"Of course, I found out from Skip later that Uncle Stephen set the whole thing up," she said, "but naturally he denied it."

Luke shook his head. "Sorry, Mom. I don't really remember him. I remember going to Florida and the beach and everything…"

(And naturally, you remember throwing up on Space Mountain, Emma thought.)

"But just not meeting this Skip guy," Luke continued. "Did we see him again after that?"

"Well, after that Skip and I sort of lost touch," she told him. "That's how it is with people, sometimes. You know…you both start living your separate lives, going your own ways."

"He lived in Florida because he was a marine biologist," she added.

"A what?" Luke asked.

"A marine biologist…someone who studies the ocean and ocean creatures and stuff," Emma explained. "Anyhow, he travels a lot…for his work, I mean, and well, after that time in Florida, we…we just kind of didn't communicate much. We live here, and you know…"

"He lives in Florida and travels a lot," Luke said.

"Right." Emma turned back toward the sink and set the plate she had just dried on the counter. Maybe it was just as well that Luke didn't remember that afternoon on the beach; it did, after all, make it easier not to have to launch into some long explanation about her and Skip. But what else was there to say, really? He was just a guy she knew when she was a kid, and no one of any consequence, as far as Luke was

8

concerned. Hell, she had friends Luke saw all the time, and he still didn't remember their names.

"Skip still sends me Christmas cards sometimes, though," she added cheerfully. But Luke had already lost interest.

"I'm going over to Zach's," he said, grabbing his jacket from the hook by the door.

"Okay, see ya," Emma said, as Luke went out the door and clomped down the back steps.

Later, when Emma pulled a cookbook off the shelf, set it on the kitchen table and began searching for something different to do with hamburger, the photograph was still there. It was true that Skip sent Christmas cards...though not every year, of course...and once in a while, a postcard from some far off place where he was busy studying something or other in some ocean...but Emma had never written back. She told herself it was because she didn't know where to write to. I mean it wasn't like the guy had any sort of permanent address. Still, maybe she could have tried a little harder along the way. After all, she had stopped being angry with him a long time ago, and bygones could easily have become bygones, if only she'd made a little effort.

"Do you ever hear from the Petersons?" Emma asked her father once, a few years after that Florida trip. At the time, he was in the garden, attempting to coax a few reluctant perennials back to life.

"The Petersons?" He asked turning to look at his daughter hesitantly.

"Yeah," Emma said, reaching down to pull a stray weed near her feet. "You know, Skip's parents? My friend from Cape Cod?"

"Oh," her father said, as he went back to gently loosening the dirt around the plants. "No, not really."

9

Then he stopped and looked up at her again.

"I guess your mother was the one who really kept up with them...actually with everyone we knew," he said. "I'm afraid I'm not as good at that...at keeping in touch with people, as good as...as she ...was..."

"I know what you mean," Emma said. "I guess I'm not so great at it either."

Now, as she sat at the old Formica table, Emma once again studied the picture of her and Skip in front of the cottage on Cape Cod, and wondered how she had let something so important slip away so easily.

Chapter Two: The Cottage on the Pond

It was in 1970 when Emma's family rented the cottage on Cape Cod for the first time. It was near the water, but then everything is near the water at that end of the Cape, so it didn't really cost any more as a result. Also, the water it was nearest to was not the wild, wavy Atlantic that chewed at the sand along Coast Guard Beach, or lashed its fury toward the Chatham Light, but was, instead, a tiny, lily-padded lake known as White Pond. Still, the cottage in Standish Village was enough to begin Emma's love affair with Cape Cod, even though she was only five years-old at the time.

Her brothers, Stephen and Joel, were ten and twelve respectively, that year, and complained bitterly about how tame the water was in the pond, how it barely rippled in the fiercest rain storms, and how it took less than three strokes to swim to the raft, and even then, you could touch bottom most of the way. But Emma didn't care what they thought. She loved the way the water gently lapped the tiny sandy beach and how the Canada Geese strutted up and down the shore, hoping for leftover bread crusts at the end of the day.

She liked it too, when her father would untie one of the rowboats, the ones that anyone could use if they were renting one of the cottages, and fasten the bulky, often soggy, red lifejacket around her waist and boost her onto the rear seat. Then he would row the two of them across the pond, reaching his long muscled arms back and forth in slow, even oar strokes until they reached the hidden cove on the other side. There he would stop and let the oars hang motionless in the silent water and both of them would sit very still.

Before long, they would appear: the tiny turtle heads popping up here and there, as the sun reflected off their armored green and brown shells; and if you watched carefully, you could see their miniature clawed feet wiggling back and forth beneath the surface of the pond, treading the water gently, as they watched Emma and her father through curious darting eyes.

She would try so hard to sit motionless, but the turtles, with their bulging eyes, their wobbling bodies, and their curious stares were just so funny, that she couldn't help but laugh. Her father would laugh with her, leaning back so far that the oars would lift out of the water and drop back in with a tremendous splash. Then, in a flurry of pops and bubbles, the turtles would abruptly vanish beneath the surface, their tiny clawed toes the last visible evidence of their presence, as they slid into the muddy bottom of the pond.

The cottage, itself, was small and rustic, with one large room sufficing for kitchen, dining and living room, and a screened porch that was close to the same size. There was one bedroom for her parents and a second for the boys, and another tiny room, probably originally intended for storage, that the owners had furnished with a narrow cot and miniature bureau. This was where Emma slept. It was much smaller than her bedroom at home, but it was cozy and cheerful, with its happy flowered quilt covering the cot and whimsical sea-themed lamp sitting on the dresser. Also, the little window in the middle of the back wall looked out on a gnarled scrub pine, where a small brown bird sat and chirped merrily every morning. This, too, made Emma happy.

But the porch was the best place in the whole cottage. Even when it was raining, she and her family could sit out there playing endless board games and watching the water drip from the pines, while never invading their screened in haven. This was because the wind invariably blew from the other direction, and the overhanging roof caught every stray shower and directed it down the rattling drain pipes in comforting vibration.

In the nice weather, it was always shady there, and while Emma's father often had to reinforce the aging screen with pieces of packing tape he cut from a huge roll (brought along just for that purpose), the mosquitos and other bugs were kept pretty much at bay in that screened-in haven.

The second summer, when Emma was six, she brought along a pile of "First Grade Readers" her mother borrowed from the library at the school where she taught. Joel, of course, made fun of her for her "baby books" (he was reading *The Count of Monte Cristo* and *Treasure Island* that summer), but Stephen, now rejected by Joel and his "teenage" friends, would sneak out onto the porch in the late afternoons and help her sound out the hard words, as she slid her finger slowly across the page.

Two years later, when Emma was eight, she swam to the raft for the first time. Her mother told her that she couldn't go out over her head until she learned to swim, that it was just "too dangerous" to be in deep water in a life jacket or tube if you couldn't swim without it. This made Emma furious, so while everyone else jumped and dove from the raft's rickety wooden surface, Emma just sat in the sand and refused to even put her toes in the water. After a while, Stephen came and sat next to her.

"I could teach you to swim, ya know," he said, as he picked up her shovel and carelessly dug in the sand by their feet.

Emma shrugged.

"Okay, I guess," she replied.

"Well," he said, "then get your butt off the sand and into the pond."

For the next hour, Stephen held her up as she floated on her back, taught her to put her face in the water and blow bubbles, float on her belly, and finally, tug her arms through the water in a defiant dog paddle. At one point, Emma looked up on the shore where her mother sat on a beach towel, ostensibly reading a book. Her mother glanced down at her and Stephen, and smiled, but Emma just ignored her and paddled even harder. Eventually, she and Stephen swam to the raft together, and all the kids who were already out there stood on the raft and cheered.

In the summer of 1975, Emma turned 10, and Joel, who was now 17 and had just gotten his driver's license, made no secret of his annoyance at having to return to that "lame cottage on that scrummy pond in Chatham" for the family's annual summer vacation. It was only when their parents allowed him to use the car while they were there, that Joel's mood improved. In fact, he even drove Emma to a special ice cream place after dinner one night, just the two of them Then, another time, he took her and Stephen to Coast Guard Beach right after a summer storm to watch the enormous waves smash the shore. He even helped Emma capture a giant conch shell that afternoon as it rolled onto the sand and nearly retreated into the foam.

But the placation of Emma's parents' eldest son, as well as his generous attitude toward his siblings, was short-lived. One Wednesday night, Joel drove a few cottage-colony-bound friends to the Wellfleet drive-in where they consumed three buckets of popcorn, six boxes of candy, and unfortunately, three six-packs of beer. On the way home, as they sang at the top of their lungs to an old Beatles song, Joel drove off the road, landing the car sideways in a ditch next to a marsh. While none of the kids inside received any substantial injuries (especially given this was a pre-seat belt era), the event flattened two tires, and caused a substantial amount of marsh muck to flow onto the seats and floorboards of the vehicle. While this final disaster resulted in an explosion of laughter from the occupants of the car, nether the police nor Emma's parents saw the humor.

It was the first time Emma ever saw her mother cry. Worse yet, her family solemnly packed up all their belongings the next morning and drove home in a rental car, a whole week early. As she sat in the backseat between her two brothers, Emma mourned the loss of her precious Cape Cod and wondered what she would do with the rest of her summer. She looked over at Stephen who was quietly gazing out the window in his usual unperturbed fashion, then turned to look at Joel.

Her eldest brother was also watching the scenery go by with casual disinterest as he rode in the silent car. He was still wearing the jeans and rumpled tee shirt from the night before, along with a muddied pair of sneakers. A thin angry line of four stitches curved over his swollen, black eye, which he squinted occasionally in the bright sunlight. Emma wondered if it hurt as badly as it appeared to and was about to ask when he turned his face in her direction, grinned slightly, and winked at her. Then, as she snuggled tentatively against him, he reached over and gently squeezed her hand.

The cut over Joel's eye healed well before school started, but the tiny white scar remained just below where he combed his dark curls as his hair grew longer. Emma's parents bought a new bright blue station wagon that had a third seat and stereo speakers in the back, which her mother turned on full blast whenever an old Beach Boys song came on the radio. Emma loved watching her mother pull off the scarf trapping her long blond hair, and shake her head happily next to the open window, as she sang along with the Wilson boys and dreamed of surfing the California coast.

In fact, everything would have been perfect if only they went back to the cottage the next summer. But her father told both of her brothers they needed to get summer jobs and save money for college, and that meant they would be working right through until school started again in the fall. One of Joel's friends got them both jobs as groundskeepers at the local golf club. This meant that Joel left for work early in the morning before Emma was awake, and came home dirty, sweaty, and exhausted before she got home from swim lessons in the afternoon. Then, by the time she was hanging her towel on the clothesline, Joel was showered, dressed, and out the door to spend the evening with his friends.

Stephen spent the summer working in the bookstore on Main Street. He told Emma that he didn't make as much money as Joel, but going there every day made him happy. He loved the smell of coffee brewing in the shop's tiny café, and Mr. Brooks, the owner, let him borrow any of the used books he wanted to, and read on his lunch hour or even bring home at the end of the day. Stephen also told Emma stories about Hemingway, Mr. Brooks' cat, who loved to sprawl in the sun in the display window, his chin resting on the latest bestseller, and

16

his tail flicking the carefully arranged posters and fliers carelessly onto the floor. Once, on his day off, Stephen took Emma to the bookstore and introduced her to Mr. Brooks and Hemingway. Mr. Brooks made her a glass of fresh-squeezed lemonade in the café and even let her ring up a customer's purchase on the ancient counter cash register.

It wasn't such a bad summer really, that year that Emma turned eleven; she swam in the town pool and had fun with her friends, and when her father took his vacation in August, she and her parents went on picnics and worked together in their huge garden. And when her parents decided to paint the house, they even let Emma help.

But she still missed Cape Cod and the little cottage on White Pond. She often wondered if the turtles still poked their inquisitive little heads up between the lily pads in the cove, or if the screens on the porch were still held together with her father's packing tape patches. Sometimes she even woke up at home in the early morning, in her big comfy bed between the large open windows in her room, and wondered who was sleeping in that narrow cot in the little cottage room, listening to the small brown bird chirping in the scrub pine outside its tiny window. What she didn't know then, was how many years would pass before her questions were answered.

Erni Johnson

Chapter Three: Standish Village (2003)

Finding out that Standish Village was for sale hadn't been easy; in fact, Emma couldn't understand how the owners planned to sell it in the first place if they didn't invest in a little better advertising. She wouldn't have known about it at all if Skip hadn't mentioned it in the note he wrote on his Christmas card.

"Can you believe that the Andersons still own Standish Village? (Skip wrote). They must be freaking old! Or maybe their kids are running it now, or something...but I remember Old Man Anderson was up there, even back in the 70s! Anyhow, the guys I used to work with down at the boatyard told me they're finally selling...I can't believe anyone even goes there anymore!"

She laughed when she read it, but nonetheless, the whole thing nagged at her all the way through January. Finally, on the 30th no less, she called a Cape Cod real estate agent she found in an old travel guide, just to see if the rumor was true. She chose the company because it had the biggest ad; a half page, in fact, with a banner that read: "Imagine Owning Your Own Business on Beautiful Cape Cod!" Underneath was a picture of a quaint, but bustling village center, and to the right of this was shot of a stately lighthouse guarding a seemingly endless stretch of sandy shore. At the bottom of the ad, in slightly smaller print, it said: "Shops, Restaurants, Motels, and Much More! Build Your Professional Future on the Shores of the Cape!

The phone rang at least a dozen times when she called, which suggested to Emma that these real estate agents must be very busy, but instead, when someone finally picked up, a sleepy sounding woman was on the other end of the line.

"Hello," she said hesitantly, then, as if confused the phone even rang in the first place quickly added, "err...umm...Parker Reality, the best place to find your place on beautiful Cape Cod!"

"Oh!" Emma said, a bit too loudly she immediately felt, "I...umm...was looking for some information about a place for sale...."

"Well, sweetheart," the woman announced cheerfully, "you most certainly called the right number then, didn't ya?"

Emma was sure she heard gum snapping.

"What I mean is," the woman added, "that's what we do here...give out information on places for sale."

Emma wasn't sure if this was sarcasm or salesmanship; after all, this wasn't something she did every day...call real estate offices, that is. She was 38 years old, and other than the years spent with her parents, Emma had never actually lived somewhere where she wasn't paying rent to someone else. She suddenly realized the conversation seemed to have ended.

"Hello?" the woman on the other end of the line inquired tentatively. More gum snapping.

"Yes, sorry," Emma said, trying to sound as mature as possible. "I heard, I mean I understand, there is a piece of property for sale that I might be interested in."

"We got lots of places you might be interested in," the woman declared cheerfully. "You lookin' for a summer place? Or a business?"

"Actually," Emma told her, "kind of both."

20

"What I mean is," she went on, when there was no response from the other end of the line, "the place...the property...I heard about, is a summer cottage colony...Standish Village, it's called."

There was more silence on the other end.

"Hello?" Emma inquired hesitantly.

"I'm going to connect you with Mr. Parker, himself," the woman replied abruptly. "Please hold."

Sounds of shuffling and muffled conversation followed and then a sudden thump that sounded like someone had dropped the receiver, more shuffling, and finally another voice came on the line, this time with a solemn and serious male tone.

"This is Ted Parker," it said, "how may I help you, Miss....?"

"Lakin," she said, "Emma Lakin."

"Miss Lakin," he repeated. "And what I can do for you today, Miss Emma Lakin?"

It seemed to Emma that Ted Parker was making a determined effort to sound, what was it, exactly? Mature? In fact, every time the man spoke, Emma could just picture him lowering his chin and pursing his lips in an attempt to make his voice sound deeper, and perhaps more adult than normal. Nonetheless, she persevered.

"I saw your ad," she said, "the one about imagining owning a business on beautiful Cape Cod."

"Ad?" Ted Parker asked.

"Yes," Emma replied, "it's right here in The Old Salt Guide, on page 32."

Once again, there was silence on the other end of the line. Emma decided to wait this one out.

"Oh," Ted Parker said, finally. "That ad."

Emma flipped back to the front cover of the travel guide she held in her hand. "August 1985" it read in the upper left hand corner. It was now January...2003.

"I...uh...think it might be an older ad," she said. It occurred to her now that she hadn't seen a copy of the Old Salt Guide in at least 15 years...but then she didn't live on the Cape after all, and that's where it was published, right?

Ted Parker seemed completely unfazed.

"And my moth...I mean, my secretary says you're interested in Standish Village?" he said. Emma thought she heard whispering in the background and the sound of someone covering the receiver with his hand.

"Well, I don't know if interested is the word," Emma said, in what she thought was her most grown-up voice. "I heard from a friend that it might be for sale and I was just wondering..."

Again her statement was met with silence.

"I was wondering if this was the case," Emma continued. "If this is true, I mean."

"Did you want to look at it?" Ted Parker suddenly blurted out.

"Look at it?" Emma asked, as she glanced down at the real estate ad she held in her hand.

"Yes," Ted Parker replied. "Look at it...tour the property..."

"And whatnot..." he added.

Emma was not entirely sure what "whatnot" meant.

"I guess so," she said. "I mean yes, I do."

"Great!" Ted Parker replied, perhaps a bit over enthusiastically, Emma observed, but then, he was a real estate agent, right? And they were supposed to be enthusiastic...at least this was her understanding, anyhow.

"When can you be here?" he asked.

"Oh!" Emma exclaimed. She hadn't thought about that aspect of the whole thing. In order to look at the property, she'd have to go there...to the Cape. She'd have to take time off from work, and then there was Luke and school...

"I...uh...maybe Friday?" she said.

"Oh, you're not here now?" Ted Parker sounded disappointed.

"Here?" Emma inquired.

"Yes," he said, "here on the Cape."

"No, no," Emma said, "I live in Upstate New York, but I've been there."

"To the Cape?" he asked.

"To Standish Village," she said, and then added, "but it was a long time ago."

"I imagine it was," Ted Parker replied.

Erni Johnson

Chapter Four: Skip

Emma and her family had been vacationing at the cottage on the White Pond for three years before Emma made a real friend there. This wasn't because there were no other kids, or even other kids close to her age, for that matter. The whole place was full of families whose offspring were all different ages, and who came there annually on vacation because of how safe it was. The little community sat well back from Route 28, the cottages lining a web of small, bumpy roadways that ran through the pines in lazy circles.

Not that you ever needed to drive anywhere, unless you were leaving Standish Village altogether, for there was also a network of neat gravel pathways that ran from cottage to cottage, and eventually down to the shores of the Pond. Even the youngest child could happily run from place to place without parental supervision, or perhaps because of it, since no matter where they were, all the parents could see all the children practically all the time.

Emma often followed the other kids down to the shuffleboard court or to the little patch of grass and dirt where everyone played croquet; and she sometimes wandered to the edge of the pond where she watched the other kids fish for perch and sunnys. But she couldn't stand to watch the fish flop and struggle for air when they were pulled from the water, so she never stayed there long. Mostly, in fact, she played by herself, which was no big deal, really; her brothers were so much older, and of course, boys, that she was used to being on her own all the time anyhow: inventing imaginary games, or practicing jump rope, or just teaching her dolls to read.

"I see you are an observer like me," was the first thing Skip said to Emma the summer they were eight. They were watching Emma's brother, Joel, and a few of his friends shoot baskets through an old netless hoop someone had nailed to the side of a storage shed. It was an especially warm afternoon in the middle of an overly hot August, and the dust from the trampled dirt beneath the players' quickly moving sneakers filled the air and coated the dry grass on which the two younger children sat. They were all impatiently waiting the obligatory hour after lunch before going back in the water, and this, in itself, sparked a number of disagreements among the players in terms of point totals.

Emma turned to look at her companion through the dusty haze.

"What's a beserver?" she asked. Even though she prided herself on having one of the best vocabularies in the third grade, she had not heard this word, and Joel always told her not to let anyone call her names.

"Someone who watches what other people do, but does not participate," Skip replied, in a tone that suggested to Emma he had memorized the definition, which in her mind was kind of a show-offy thing to do. But when he glanced over at her, he simply smiled and added cautiously "maybe that means we could be friends."

"Okay," Emma replied. And that was that.

Over the next two weeks, Emma and Skip became inseparable, as they swam, dug in the sand, tossed bread crusts to the feisty geese, and devoured the burnt marshmallows they discovered they both loved.

Emma soon learned that "Skip" was short for his real name, Frank, which of course, made no sense to Emma at first, until she learned that Frank was also Skip's father's name. Her mother explained to her that this was a nickname used to "Skip" the confusion this situation caused. She also found out that Skip had three older sisters, and therefore, his family rented the largest cottage on the property, which was right next door to the one where Emma's family stayed.

Skip's sisters all wore identical two piece bathing suits and flowered bathing caps from which identical red curls struggled to escape. They usually shared a giant beach towel in the patch of sand by the shore, and spent most of every afternoon painting their toenails weird colors or giggling over the pile of movie magazines they brought with them to the beach. One of them was always hugging Skip and mussing his hair, or asking in loud tones where his "little girlfriend" was.

But Skip didn't seem to mind. In fact, he didn't seem to mind much of anything. When his sisters teased him or splashed water on him, he just shrugged and smiled, and when they simply ignored him in favor of each other, Skip just found something else to do. But what Emma liked most about Skip was that he always seemed to know exactly what she was thinking or how she was feeling before she even told him.

"I know just how you feel," he said abruptly, the minute he sat down next to her at one of the community bonfires. As it happened, it was the night before her family was supposed to leave for home, and Emma had been nearly inconsolable since she woke up that morning. Then in the usual way in which Skip resolved every troubling issue, he added, "my sister, Eleanor, has a pen pal she met two years ago at camp. They never see each other, but they write letters all the time."

"Maybe," he continued firmly, "we could be pen pals."

And so, they were. Not just that school year, but for many more, even when Emma's family stopped going to Standish Village, after the summer Joel wrecked the family car.

"It's really lonely here without you," Skip wrote that first summer when Emma wasn't there. "But I plan on making new friends."

At first Emma was mad at him for saying that and didn't write to him again for quite a while, but then Emma's mother heard from Skip's mother that he just "moped around for weeks without his favorite playmate." Emma wondered later if her mother just made that up, but it was enough to make her finally write back, something she was always glad she did.

"We're going to Washington DC this summer instead of going back to the Cape," Skip wrote her, the year they both turned twelve. A few months later he wrote her a long letter describing all the museums they toured, and how they went to the White House and even shook hands with Jimmy Carter (though Emma wasn't convinced this was true). He also sent her a sort of fuzzy gray picture of the Washington Monument that he took with his "Polaroid," whatever that was. "But I still miss 'that old Cape Cod'," he wrote, "and 'eating lobster stew by a window with an ocean view'."

Hard as she tried to remember, Emma could not think of a single time that she and Skip had ever eaten lobster stew together, much less by a window with an ocean view. This made her wonder if he really did make new friends and this was something he did with them. Later, though, Emma found out that Skip had put this in quotes

28

because it was a line from some 50s song by someone named Patti Page. She tried to find a copy of the record in the music store downtown, but the teenage sales clerk didn't seem to know what she was talking about.

"Patti Page?" the clerk said crinkling his nose as if he smelled some foul odor. "Why would you want to listen to something by that old bag? We got the new Rolling Stones single in this week, if you want to check that out."

But Emma wasn't interested. She just wanted to find that Cape Cod song and planned to keep looking until she did.

Erni Johnson

Chapter Five: Road Trip (2003)

As it turned out, Emma didn't meet with the real estate agent until two months after they originally spoke. First, Luke's basketball team made it to the finals, then there were midterm exams for both of them (hers to give and grade, his to take), then her landlord announced he was selling the house they were renting, and Emma had to start looking for a new place to live. It wasn't until March vacation, therefore, that she finally called Ted Parker to set up an appointment.

"I hope the property is still available," she said to the agent on the phone.

"Absolutely!" Ted Parker exclaimed.

It seemed odd to Emma at the time that he didn't even have to look it up, but she pushed the thought aside.

"How about sometime next week?" the real estate agent suggested.

"Perfect," Emma replied.

"We're going where on break?" Luke asked, when Emma told him of her plans.

"Cape Cod," she remarked cheerfully. At the time, she was staring into a kitchen cupboard wondering where all those glasses came from, and more importantly, how long it would take her to pack them all up. Luke was currently drinking juice directly from the bottle.

"No offense, Mom," he said, between gulps, "but isn't that somewhere you go in the summer? I was thinking maybe Florida or something. I mean we do have that money from Gramps...maybe we could even take a real vacation to some island somewhere."

"We'll do that too," she assured him, "or at least on the next vacation. This time I have to go to the Cape for a few days...on business."

"Business?" Luke demanded, as he recapped the juice and shoved it onto an already crowded refrigerator shelf. "What business? You're a teacher."

"Maybe I don't want to be a teacher forever," she told him.

"What?" he teased. "And give up all that exceptional pay? Not to mention the opportunity to embarrass your son by your daily presence at his school?"

"But whatever you're planning," he added, smiling, "I'm in."

"All for one," Emma said.

"And one for all," Luke replied.

She had to admit it was still nice to hear him repeat their old inside joke, especially since he'd been a bit more distant lately. If only Luke knew what he was getting into, Emma thought, but then decided it might be better that he didn't.

The calendar declared it was the first day of spring when she and Luke tossed their bags into her aging Jeep Wrangler the morning they left for the Cape, but as Emma stepped outside and zipped up her winter parka it certainly didn't feel that way. Several stubborn piles of gray snow still sat along the edge of the driveway, and the tree limbs were still black and bare in the morning sun. Nonetheless, a few birds chirped from their leafless domain overhead and the sky struggled toward blue.

"So, tell me again where this place is?" Luke asked, as Emma backed the car into the street. He was sitting on the passenger side with a map of New England unfolded in his lap, running his finger across the nearest highway line.

"It's on Cape Cod," she said, "which if you unfold that map a little farther, is way over on the right edge. See that chunk of land kind of shaped like an arm? Where we're going is right around what looks like the elbow."

Luke turned the map slightly and then refolded it so the part in front of him appeared to be mostly ocean.

"Here?" he asked pointing to where a narrow peninsula left the edge of the solid looking Massachusetts shoreline and twisted upward until it ended across a small stretch of water from Boston.

Emma glanced over at the map.

"Yup," she said, "that's it."

"How do we get there?" her son asked. "I mean is there a bridge from Boston or something? Because I don't see one."

"You don't get there from Boston," Emma told him. "You have to go way down to the south, where that piece of land starts, and go across a bridge there."

"Well that's kind of dumb," Luke remarked. "Seems like it would be smarter to build a bridge from Boston...it looks like going way down there, and then all the way back up to that elbow you're talking about is really out of the way."

"That's what makes it so nice," Emma said, as she pulled out on the main road and threw the jeep into third gear.

Luke shrugged.

"If you say so," he said.

By the time they stopped for lunch at the beginning of the Mass
Pike, the sky had turned a dull gray and every now and then, a random
gust of wind blew a cloud of leftover sand and road salt across the
windshield. The rest area was fairly deserted as a bored looking,
pimply-faced teenager, with clearly better things to do, shoved their
McDonald's order across the counter.

"Thanks," Emma said, not really meaning it, as she held out her
hand, waiting for her change. The kid stared at her briefly, before
dropping her a dime and three pennies into her palm with an
exaggerated sigh.

"Have a good day," he muttered.

"I think he might have been expecting a tip," Luke suggested, as
he carried their tray toward a vacant table by the window.

"Yeah," Emma replied, "I got a tip for him…"

"Stay in school, kid," they both said at the same time, and
laughed.

"Thanks for coming along," Emma said, as they settled in their
seats and began to unwrap the poor excuse for burgers.

"Did I have a choice?" Luke teased as he took a large bite of his
Big Mac and threw a few French fries in his mouth for good measure.

"You could have gone on the buying trip with Uncle Stephen,"
Emma said, as she picked cautiously at her lunch, "or with Uncle Joel
and his little girls to Hershey Park."

Emma opened her hamburger roll and peered inside.

"Oh Mom," Luke said, slapping the top of her roll back over its contents, "don't do that! You'll never eat be able to eat it if you see what's inside."

"And thanks so much for both those truly generous offers," he added, "but I think even this (he gestured vaguely around the room), trumps those other fine opportunities."

"Suit yourself," Emma said solemnly, but when she looked up from her lunch, Luke was grinning at her.

By late afternoon they had reached the Sagamore Bridge. Beneath them, the canal swirled and lapped its way between the bay and the ocean, as the gradually retreating tide revealed the sculpted rocky shore along its edge. A small red tugboat determinedly dragged an oversized barge through the center of the waterway, large puffs of brown smoke escaping from its battered stack, as it strained against a seemingly impossible task. Even the air appeared to have taken on a grayish hue, despite the tiny rays of sun attempting to penetrate its solemn thickness.

Someone had tied a bouquet of flowers to one of the rails on the bridge, and a lone seagull was now perched precariously next to the memorial, pecking tentatively at the arrangement. Emma glanced briefly at the bird, as bits of dried greenery and frozen flower remnants strayed across her windshield. Then she looked over at her son.

Luke had refolded the map somewhat chaotically, dropping it on the floor by his feet, and was now staring straight ahead, silently absorbed in the endless stretch of road in front of them.

"So, Mom," he said at last, as they bumped their way off the bridge and onto Route 6, "what if you see this place, this Standish Village, and decide you're going to buy it, what then?"

35

"What do you mean, what then?" Emma asked. "Then I'll own the place and I'll run it...you know, it'll be my business, my job."

"You already have a job," Luke remarked, somewhat sullenly it seemed to Emma.

"Okay, then," she replied evenly, "it'll be my new job."

"Do you even know anything about running a motel?" he asked, turning his head in her direction.

"Cottage colony," Emma said. Right at that moment she was happy to have to keep her eyes on the road as a large delivery truck pulled in front of her, swaying dangerously back and forth.

"What?" Luke asked.

"Cottage colony," Emma repeated. "It's not a motel, it's a cottage colony. Thus the name, Village, Standish *Village*."

"Whatever," Luke said.

They rode in silence for a few minutes.

"I guess what I'm asking," he said at last, "is what happens to me? To us? To our lives?"

Emma wasn't sure how to answer. If the truth be known, she hadn't really thought much about this. In fact, she wasn't really sure why she was doing this in the first place...driving all the way out to Cape Cod to look at this cottage colony, to consider buying it, for heaven's sake, and then? Luke was right. And then what happens?

"I don't know," she said finally, because truthfully, she just didn't.

Chapter Six: Reunion (1980)

The summer Emma turned 15, her mother announced they were going to visit Skip's family; not in New Jersey where his family actually lived, but on Cape Cod, where Skip's parents had recently bought a vacation home. It would just be the three of them going, her mother explained: Emma and her parents, as neither of her brothers would be able to join them. Joel, after several fruitless attempts at college, was now working construction for a friend's father's company, and Stephen, a fine arts major at Boston College, had already left for Italy to start his junior year abroad a few months early.

In fact, Emma's mother told her, they had all been invited to Skip's oldest sister, Anna's wedding which was taking place in Chatham the week they were going to be there.

"It seems like the perfect chance to take another Cape vacation, don't you think?" Emma's father asked her hopefully. "We've been wanting to go back there for years!"

Then why didn't we? Emma wondered at the time, but thought better of asking. She was just happy her parents were so enthusiastic about the trip, even if she was a little apprehensive about seeing Skip again after so many years. What if he wasn't the same? Or worse yet, what if he looked at her and decided they weren't really friends after all, she thought, as she stood staring in her bedroom mirror the day before they left.

Even though she and Skip had been penpals all this time, the last time they'd actually been together, they were barely 10 years old. In those days, she was just a little kid with messy blond pigtails and red Keds; a silly girl who loved eating burnt marshmallows and catching fireflies in old jelly jars. Now, when she stared in the mirror, she saw a skinny teenage girl looking back at her, her dull brownish hair pulled back in a careless braid, and several new pimples sprouting under her bangs and across the bridge of her nose. In his last letter, Skip had talked about his lacrosse team and the car he was saving up to buy; Emma was pretty sure he'd be less than impressed with the second hand bike she'd been riding to school, not to mention her new position as the yearbook photographer.

"Anna's wedding will be a necessary evil," Skip had written earlier that week, "but we can probably sneak some champagne, and later I can introduce you to my friends at the beach! We'll have a bonfire and burn marshmallows just like we used to in the old days!"

Though she was encouraged by what seemed like sentimental enthusiasm on his part, Emma still had her doubts about the whole trip.

"You don't seem too excited for a girl off to see her childhood sweetheart!" her father teased as they packed the car together.

"Dad, please," Emma sighed, "he's just an old friend...a friend I haven't seen for five years. We probably won't have anything to say to each other after all this time."

"Hmm..." he replied, yanking her braid affectionately, "that's not what I hear."

Even though Emma had not seen Skip, her parents and his parents had met for weekends in New York City several times since they all spent their summer vacations together at Standish Village.

Meanwhile she stayed home with her brothers, and he with his sisters, and the idea that there had been conversation about her and Skip on those occasions was too embarrassing to even think about.

"Whatever," Emma told her father, hoping she was casual enough in her response to end the discussion.

The trip to the Cape seemed endless and Emma tried her best to look absorbed in the book she brought along. Even so, she would occasionally catch her father peering back at her in the rear view mirror, or her mother nonchalantly turning to glance over her shoulder and then smiling expectantly. And as if this, in itself, wasn't bad enough, by the time they checked into their hotel and met Skip's parents for dinner, Skip had already gone off to a party with his friends.

"I apologize for my son's apparent rudeness," Mr. Peterson told Emma, "but it seems a plan was made to celebrate his lacrosse team winning the championship, and well, they did!"

"You should have seen that game!" he went on, turning to Emma's father and proceeding to give a blow by blow description of the final moments of the match, one that had apparently taken place in New Jersey that afternoon right before the Peterson family raced to the Cape for Anna's wedding. But Emma didn't care. She decided at that moment that the whole visit with Skip's family was just something to be endured, and that soon she'd be back home with her real friends doing the usual summer stuff. If Skip was at some Lacrosse party in New Jersey that night, he'd probably just barely get here in time for his sister's wedding the next afternoon. As Emma picked at her dinner and flashed periodic fake smiles at her parents and the Petersons, she tried hard to convince herself that it really didn't matter where Skip was or when he'd be on the cape.

The next morning when her parents went off on a sightseeing adventure with the Petersons, Emma told them she was tired and asked if she could just hang out by the hotel pool. Her mother looked concerned, but finally agreed, and soon Emma was alone on a lounger with only her book and her Walkman to keep her company.

"Are you purposefully avoiding me?" he said, as he plopped down in the chair next to hers, "or did you just forget I was even going to be on the Cape this week?"

Emma lowered her sunglasses and turned to look at her new companion.

"Are those my only choices?" she asked, "because, in that case, I may have to think it over."

Even with the glare of the sun on his face, Skip was still the same red-haired freckle-faced ten-year-old she remembered; taller certainly, and with just a shadow of whiskers on his chin and upper lip, but the same lopsided grin spread across his face.

"Besides," Emma added, as she shaded her eyes with her hand, "do I even know you? I'm not supposed to talk to strangers."

"Oh dear," Skip replied mockingly, as he leaned back on his lounger, "I'm so sorry Miss, you just looked like someone I used to know. An old friend I was thinking of asking to lunch, actually."

"Well," Emma said, "I *am* pretty hungry."

"Okay, then," he said, "forget the old friend. How about you and I just go and eat lunch then?"

"Sounds good," she declared, as she stood and gathered her belongings. "Who cares about that old friend, anyhow?"

If anyone were to ask her what she considered the best day of her life thus far, Emma would have immediately answered it was this one; although at 15, one's experience might be limited, but Emma didn't care. She wanted to revel in the feeling of simply being part of that August afternoon and sharing it with Skip.

At first, they just walked into town, and bought clam strips, which they shared on a rickety old picnic table next to the town parking lot. They talked about school and friends, and all the things teenagers consider vital to existence. But three short hours later, they found themselves on the wide and wild section of the beach just below the protective beam of Chatham light, sitting silently on a gentle sandy rise and staring out to sea.

"Where do you see yourself in fifteen years?" Skip asked Emma abruptly. He had picked up a small piece of tangled driftwood earlier as they walked along the beach, and was now dragging it slowly through the sand between them, creating large circular patterns around their buried toes.

"What do you mean, where do I see myself?" Emma turned and studied the profile of the boy next to her. She felt like he was someone she knew inside and out, like he was a part of herself, but at the same time, he was suddenly a stranger, mysteriously hidden beneath the chaotic red curls and familiar lopsided grin.

"It's a question we had to write about at school this year," Skip explained. "One of those exercises that supposedly produces a 'sense of self'."

As he said this, he lifted his hands and made quotation marks in the air.

"It's a college prep thing," he added, "you know, for when you have to write a personal statement or describe your goals or whatever on a college application."

Emma stretched her legs out lazily in front of her, wiggling her toes to knock off the sand stubbornly clinging to them.

"I don't know if I've ever thought about that," she said finally.

"Yeah," Skip replied, "that's what most of the kids said...either that or they just sat there griping about how lame the whole thing was."

"Lame?" Emma asked.

"Right," he said. "You know, like why would anyone ask this in the first place? My friend, Keith, even said something like, 'I don't even know what I'm doing tomorrow.'"

Emma laughed.

"Typical guy," she joked.

"Yeah, well, I thought it was pretty funny at the time too," Skip said, smiling. "Everyone did. But then later, when we had to go home and write the answer for homework, I suddenly started thinking about the whole thing more."

"And what did you come up with?" Emma asked.

"Come up with?" Skip said.

"Yeah, where did you decide you saw yourself? You know, fifteen years from now."

"It was a little creepy, actually," Skip admitted.

"Creepy?" Emma said.

"Yeah," Skip insisted. "I mean, at first, I came up with all these scenarios...you know...like what kind of job I would have, or where I would live, whether I'd be married and have kids and all that..."

"And?"

"And I just couldn't make it work," he went on. "It wasn't exactly like I couldn't see myself doing any of those regular things, but that I couldn't see myself anywhere at all."

42

"That *is* pretty creepy," Emma admitted, though what she really wanted to say was that she had pretty much the same feeling herself.

"Maybe it's just because you haven't made a definite plan yet," she suggested. "Like you need to think about it some more...or you want to wait and see where life takes you first. Like you don't think that you should make that plan until you have more...I don't know... experience ...or something."

"So?" Skip said, "your turn. Now you tell me where you'll be fifteen years from now and what you'll be doing."

Emma looked back out at the waves, rising, cresting, and then rushing across the sandbar at the mouth of the tiny inlet below. Overhead a seagull swooped lazily in the breeze and then hung suspended over the beach. Suddenly the gull plunged to the shoreline where the tide had begun to recede, and grasping a clam shell in its beak soared quickly back over their heads and disappeared.

"Okay, I'll play," Emma said. Then pulling her knees up to her chest, she wrapped her arms around her legs and rested her chin on top.

"I won't be married, I'll tell you that much," she declared.

"No?" Skip leaned back in mock horror.

"Absolutely not," Emma replied firmly. "And definitely no kids yet...I'll only be 30, and I will have had to get my career off the ground before all that!"

"All that?" Skip exclaimed.

Emma reached her foot over and kicked him playfully.

"Now you're just making fun of me," she said.

43

"Well," he replied, "you really haven't answered the question. I mean what is this great career that you have to get off the ground? That's what I really want to know."

Emma shrugged.

"I guess I haven't figured that out yet," she said. "I have to go to college first, don't I? To find out what I want to do, I mean...and then spend a few years out in the working world, you know, trying things out?"

"I guess," Skip replied hesitantly.

"Don't tell me you already know what you want to do," Emma said. "How is that even possible? You're not even sixteen."

Skip stood and brushed the sand off his legs.

"A marine biologist," he stated firmly.

"What?" Emma asked as she stood up next to him.

"I want to be a marine biologist," Skip repeated. "It's what I always wanted to do...only before I went to career day at school, I didn't know what it was called."

"What do marine biologists do?" Emma inquired, in what she hoped was her most respectful voice. Somehow, she wanted Skip to understand how supportive she was being, how receptive she was to his dreams and goals...or something like that.

"They study the sea," he explained, "and all sorts of sea life...like to protect it, preserve it...you know, make sure we don't forget where we came from."

Emma thought he sounded like he was quoting a brochure, but she didn't tell him that. Instead she asked, "what do your parents think?"

"I didn't tell them yet," Skip said.

"How come?"

"I don't know," he said. "Maybe because every time I bring up something I might want to do with my life, my Dad always says, 'Well Son, you never know what's around the next corner...'"

Emma giggled at the mock seriousness with which Skip imitated his father's voice.

"You kinda sound just like him," she teased, and Skip started to laugh as well. But something told Emma that Mr. Peterson might be right, and for some reason, this realization made her feel very sad.

Chapter Seven: The Bandstand (2003)

By the time she and Luke reached the Inn, it was nearly dark, but Emma still felt the welcoming sense of familiarity when she drove down the main street of Chatham. Oh, certainly the town had changed since the last time she was here; new boutiques and upscale restaurants lined the sidewalks where clam shacks and cheap souvenir stores once stood. But the evidence of historic cobblestones still disrupted the now paved surface of the street, and the storefronts were still shaded with the old-fashioned striped awnings they had always worn.

Emma pulled the car into the nearly deserted parking lot, opened her door and stepped out. Overhead the sky was darkening to that dull shade of blue she remembered so well, as all around them the streetlights began to softly glow.

"Listen to that, Luke," she said. Her son, having untangled his long legs from under the passenger side dashboard, had climbed out of the car and was already pulling their duffle bags from the back of the vehicle. He stopped and stood silently.

"Listen to what?" he asked. "I don't hear anything."

"Exactly," Emma declared. "Listen to the silence! Isn't it heavenly?"

Luke stood behind the car with one hand poised over their luggage.

"Yeah, Mom," he replied finally, and then grinning mischievously, added, "heavenly."

At that moment, a lone seagull flew across the sky above them, cawing loudly as he was quickly silhouetted by the rays of the setting sun.

"Now that," Luke said, as he tugged at the handle of a reluctant duffle, "is worth listening to."

"It certainly is," Emma agreed.

The next morning, while Luke was still asleep, Emma slipped out the back door of the inn into the garden that stretched along one side of the old clapboard building and then meandered casually behind the stores lining Main Street. Most of the plants were dormant, their brown stalks chopped back in the fall before the insistent wave of nor'easters buried them in winter whiteness. But here and there, Emma caught a glimpse of a tiny green sprout struggling to reclaim possession of its patch of still unbroken soil. Soon, she thought, the path on which she walked would be lined with color, and the flowers would once more be waving back and forth in the ocean breeze.

There was something about returning to Cape Cod before this happened that made Emma feel as though she were in the possession of a shared secret; something only she and the early sprouts of spring knew and no one else finding their way to the edge of the sea long after the sun had grown strong and hot, would ever quite understand.

At the end of the path, the garden opened out into a wide grassy area in the center of which stood the old town bandstand. When she and her brothers were kids, Emma's parents used to bring them here on Sunday nights to hear concerts performed by the town band: a group of middle-aged men who during the week were shop owners or innkeepers, and perhaps even doctors or lawyers. But on Sunday nights, these men donned their worn blue uniforms and tuned their well-used instruments, bringing the fading day to a close with the consoling sound of well-known tunes and soulful melodies of the past.

Emma remembered how her parents used to like it when the band struck up a romantic 60s tune, while her brothers used to roll on the ground laughing whenever the group attempted to play a Beatles song. As for Emma, her fondest memories were when the band launched into its own unique rendition of "The Bunny Hop." As soon as the first few notes played, adults and kids alike would jump up from their picnic blankets and form a circle around the bandstand, hands on the shoulders or waist of the person in front of them and start to hop...forward, backward, forward hop, hop, hop...all in time to the rhythm of the drums and horns, and the cheerful voice of the band leader as he called out the movements. Then, as the August twilight settled over the hopping, laughing circle of families, the music would slowly fade and everyone would clap and cheer for an encore.

Emma wasn't sure why she liked this part of the concerts so much; in general, she tended to be a shy, contemplative child, who usually hung back from these gregarious displays of camaraderie. But there was something about doing "The Bunny Hop" that made you feel like you were part of something fun and exciting, and yet uniquely inclusive; as if everyone dancing suddenly became your friends ...welcoming, non-critical friends, who simply took you as you were, with a kind of unconditional acceptance. Perhaps, Emma thought, as she wandered near the steps of the old, paint-peeling structure and began to unconsciously hum the "Bunny Hop" tune, it was because it had been so many years since she felt that sense of belonging or experienced that kind of natural affection.

"Ah, the infamous Bunny Hop," came a voice from the other side of the steps. "It's been a long time since I heard that one!"

Startled, Emma peered cautiously around the edge of the bandstand platform. On the grass next to the steps, knelt a somewhat elderly man, who squinted up at Emma from underneath the brim of a spattered painter's cap. The hat was pulled down firmly on his head, probably to avoid being tugged away by the morning sea breeze, but also something which caused large tuffs of shaggy white hair to bulge over the tops of his ears from within.

"Oh, sorry, miss," the man said, as he studied the surprised expression on Emma's face, "I guess you weren't expectin' to see someone workin' here."

"Just paintin' the old bandstand before the season starts," he added, unnecessarily it seemed to Emma, since the man was also wearing a pair of canvas overalls spotted with a veritable pallet of colors, and held a thick paintbrush, dripping globs of white paint.

A wide grin slowly spread beneath his bushy white mustache as he grabbed the stair railing and struggled to his feet, the dripping paint brush still dangling from one hand. For the life of her, Emma could not see any evidence that the man had even begun the painting project, nor could she locate the can of paint in which it appeared he had only recently dipped his brush.

"Does the band still play on Sunday nights?" Emma asked, in part to cover the fact that she may have been staring at the man rather rudely.

The painter turned and looked up the steps leading to the bandstand itself; then he scratched his chin and silently studied the platform.

50

"I expect they still do," he said at last. "Don't know for sure, though, it not being summer yet and all."

Then he set the paintbrush on the steps, wiped his hand on his overalls, and held it out in her direction.

"Name's Charlie," he said.

"Emma," Emma replied, reaching over and shaking his outstretched hand.

"You live around here?" Charlie asked. "I don't remember seein' you before."

"No," Emma said. "At least not yet."

"What I mean is," she continued, "maybe I will...soon...but not now, no."

Charlie continued to study her carefully and then grinned again.

"Okay," he remarked cheerfully, and turned to pick up the brush once more.

"What I meant is," Emma added hastily, fearing she had offended the man somehow, "I'm staying here at the inn...with my son...he's still asleep."

Charlie nodded.

"And well, I actually came here...to Chatham, that is...to look at some property...to buy...a business, actually," she went on quickly. "So, I might live here...be from here...soon."

Charlie nodded again.

"And I know about the Bunny Hop," Emma blurted awkwardly, "because I used to come here in the summers when I was a kid...and my parents always brought us here on Sundays and well, seeing the bandstand again reminded me of that song...and you know, hopping around it."

Emma stopped to catch her breath and then smiled shyly. Charlie smiled back as they both stood there briefly, staring at each other.

"I guess I should let you get back to work," Emma said finally. "And Luke, that's my son, he's probably awake and wondering where I am."

But Charlie didn't seem to hear her.

"That sure was fun," he said, leaning back and looking up toward the bandstand again. "We loved playing that song, and just seeing everyone join in, even if they were total strangers!"

"We?" Emma thought. What did he mean by "we?"

"Were you in the town band?" she asked.

Charlie looked back at her and chuckled.

"Oh, for a few years," he told her, "back in the 70s. It was...a long time ago...you might not recall those days."

Then he leaned down and picked up a bucket of paint that seemed to have suddenly materialized in the grass nearby.

"Long time ago," he repeated, and then turned and started to walk down the path in the opposite direction.

"But..." she called after him, "that's when I was here...in the 70s...and I came here...to the bandstand..."

"Nice meetin' ya, Miss Emma," he called over his shoulder. "I sure do hope you decide to stay...here on old Cape Cod, that is."

"Stay?" she said, "but I haven't even...I mean I don't know if I want..."

But Charlie didn't seem to hear her and before she could decide to follow him, he disappeared around the corner of the next building and vanished from sight.

She stood there for a moment, contemplating this strange encounter. What did he mean, he hoped she'd decide to stay? Why would that be any concern of his, someone she didn't even know? And what did he mean by "old Cape Cod?" The expression struck her as somehow familiar, but she could place how...or from where.

Oh well, she thought, as she turned back towards the inn, where the early morning bustle of breakfast preparations could now be heard, if there's one thing I know about the Cape, it's that there are plenty of old timers out here, and they all think it's the only place to be.

It didn't strike Emma until much later, long after she'd walked back through the garden, into the inn, and woke Luke ...and, in fact, not until after they were sitting downstairs in the dining room eating breakfast...that she had not witnessed Charlie actually painting the bandstand.

Erni Johnson

Chapter Eight: Anna's Wedding (1980)

Anna's wedding was an elegant affair during which 15 year-old Emma felt mostly underdressed and out of place. She thought her parents displayed a similar wardrobe issue and yet they didn't seem to notice. The three of them were given the honor of being seated at the same table as the bride's parents, which seemed to be a delightful experience for the adults, but made Emma simply feel smaller and less significant than she had in the first place. Skip, meanwhile, being one of the groomsmen, sat at the head table, looking completely at home in his white tux, as he sipped nonchalantly from his champagne glass.

At the cocktail hour prior to dinner, Skip had indeed acquainted Emma with his friends (those who had accompanied their parents to the event), including a tall, slim girl with impossibly shiny black hair who introduced herself as "Caitlin with C," while laying her hand possessively on Skip's arm. It wasn't until the cake was cut and the DJ started the dance music, that Emma was able to escape the adult conversation by casually making her way to the dessert buffet; not that she thought loading up on sugar would make this evening any better, but at least she would be able to stop nodding and smiling inanely for a few minutes, and pretend to make an after dinner choice instead.

Despite the drunken laughter of the bridesmaids dancing to "Maggie May" in the background, Emma had to admit, as she hovered near the dessert table, that the wedding was something out of a fairy tale. The tiny old church in the middle of Chatham had been packed with guests, literally squashed into the historic wooden pews, the ends of which were decorated with huge white silk bows and bouquets of tiny red roses.

Then, when the old pipe organ in the loft overhead burst into the wedding march, the bridesmaids with their pink silk dresses and bouquets of crisp flowers slowly glided down the aisle ahead of Anna and her father. And the bride herself! How did that flowered two-pieced, tousle-haired, red-headed child of Emma's youth transform into the elegant bride who now moved so gracefully toward the altar? In some ways, it felt hopeful to Emma...like everyone, no matter what their childhood awkwardness, could have their own fairy tales in the end.

"Wanna get out of here?" a low male voice over her left shoulder whispered hoarsely.

Startled, Emma nearly dropped the delicate china dessert plate she had just selected from the pile, and turning her head cautiously, she found herself face to face with a drunkenly grinning Skip.

"Seriously?" Emma inquired, as she gestured vaguely in the direction of the wedding festivities. "Don't you have some groomsmanly duties you need to attend to?"

"Nah," Skip replied shaking his head, "that's pretty much over with, plus my parents have started watching me a little too closely."

"Why?" Emma asked.

Skip shrugged.

"Who knows?" he said. "Maybe I'm looking a bit bored, and to them, that's always a danger signal."

"Right," Emma said. "Been there. I have two brothers, remember?"

"One of whom, also, right now," she added, "is alone in my house in Albany."

"So how come your parents don't look worried?" Skip asked, nodding in the direction of the crowded reception.

"I'm thinking they've given up," Emma said and smiled.

"So, what and where did you have in mind?" she asked. "For the wanna get out of here thing, I mean?"

Skip shrugged again.

"I don't know," he said, then gestured toward a nearby exit sign, "there's a beach out yonder."

"Sounds good to me," Emma said.

"Oh and..." Skip added, "I do have this."

Then pulling his hand out from behind his back, he held up a bottle of champagne.

"Even better," Emma declared, and together they quietly slipped out the back door of the wedding venue.

Compared with the music and laughter of the reception, the moonlit beach seemed unusually quiet when Skip and Emma reached the end of the hidden pathway. A few stalwart gulls prowled the water's edge searching for the remains of the outgoing tide's harvest, but otherwise the beach was empty and the only sound was of the miniature bayside waves gently lapping the shoreline.

Skip removed his tux jacket and tossed it on the sand, then sat down on top of it and patted the space next to him.

"Are you sure?" Emma said. "That's a pretty nice tux. Won't you get sand all over it?"

Skip shrugged.

"And in the pockets and everything," he said, idly brushing the sleeve to his right. "It is, however, rented, and if I return it coated with beach sand, it will give Fred and Herman something to talk about."

"Fred and Herman?" Emma asked as she sat down next to him.

"Yeah," Skip replied, lying back and staring up at the sky. "Those are the guys in the tux rental place, and trust me when I tell you they really need something to talk about...other than bowties and cummerbunds, I mean."

Emma laughed.

"Skip Peterson," she exclaimed, "that's just plain mean."

"Okay," he said, "but seriously, I think they live there...in the tux store, I'm saying. Neither one look like they have seen a single ray of sunlight for the last 20 years."

"Well," Emma remarked, as she, too, lay back and stared upward, "not everyone has the opportunity to become a bronze beach god every summer...some people even have to work."

"Hey!" Skip said, turning his head in Emma's direction, "I work!"

"Oh sure," Emma scoffed, "is that what you call it? Hanging out down at the marina and polishing your boat, while you wait for someone to come and pay you to give them a ride to theirs?"

"Not to mention having Caitlin with a C keeping you company all day..." she added. Then she smirked slightly and closed her eyes. When she opened them again, Skip was propped on one elbow staring at her.

"And just how did you come by this information?" he demanded.

"I will never divulge my sources," Emma replied and closed her eyes again.

They both lay there silently for a few minutes, then Skip sat up abruptly.

"You know what's wrong with us lying here like this?" he asked.

"Other than creating the mystery of the sandy tuxedo jacket for Fred and Herman to ponder?" Emma said, her eyes still closed.

"No, I mean you and me lying here on the sand, listening to the waves, and looking up at the moon," Skip said softly.

Emma opened her eyes and turned to look at him.

"What?" she asked cautiously.

"We can't drink this," Skip announced, holding up the bottle of champagne, "if we're lying down."

Then with a resounding pop, he uncorked the bottle and passed it to Emma.

"Sorry," he said, "forgot the champagne glasses."

"No problem," Emma replied and pulling herself up to a sitting position, she removed the bottle from Skip's outstretched hand, tipped it back, and took one long fizzy gulp.

Chapter Nine: Cottages For Sale (2003)

When Emma drove into Standish Village that afternoon, Ted Parker had yet to arrive. The off-season quiet in town was emphasized further by the eerie stillness of the empty cottage colony at the bottom of the long winding drive in front of her.

"Are you sure you don't want me to come?" Luke had asked as he peered out from under the crumpled bed covers earlier that morning and yawned lazily. "I mean, are you sure you even know where this place is?"

"It'll be fine," Emma assured him, "and after all, this is your vacation too, so it seems like you should have some time to yourself...you know, to just relax."

"In fact," she added, as she pulled a bulky sweater over her head, "why don't you take a walk down to the lighthouse? There's a beautiful wild beach down there where the seals hang out when no one's around. You brought your camera, right?"

"Never leave home without it," Luke said, as he stretched his arms over his head and yawned again.

Photography was Luke's latest interest, and as a result, Emma's brother, Joel, had bought him a new Minolta complete with filters and lenses as a Christmas gift. Personally, Emma suspected that Joel just did this as a way to flash his big salary around, but she did her best to smile graciously for Luke's sake; besides the kid really did love that camera, and maybe he truly needed something like this right now to focus on. After all, he had just lost his beloved grandfather, and though Luke didn't talk about his feelings much, Emma could tell that the empty spot in his life was as big as the one in hers.

"I thought you said the appointment with that real estate guy wasn't until later," Luke said, as he swung his legs out from under the covers and headed toward the bathroom.

"It isn't," Emma replied, as she picked up her purse and keys from the bedside table, "but I have a few errands to run first...you know, pick up some snacks for later and stuff..."

But Luke had already closed the bathroom door and started brushing his teeth.

"See ya in a while," she called.

"Yup," he said. Then Emma heard the shower go on and that was that.

While the sign itself was visible from the road, it wasn't until she drove into the actual property that its faded blue lettering was even slightly legible. And even then, when the letters came more fully into view, it was hard to decipher the specific words. Added to this was the fact that, because one of the posts holding the decaying wooden structure in place had rotted, one also had to bend down and look up into its now tilted surface to have any chance of doing so.

Instead of attempting this, however, Emma got out of her car and walked down the driveway to the top of the hill overlooking the cottage complex. Granted it was off season, but there was something remarkably silent about the scene below. And a little spooky, Emma thought, but immediately pushed the idea aside. After all, the cottages looked much the same as Emma remembered them, despite being weathered by time, and the little road that meandered between them was still gently coated with the crisp brown needles that fell from the enveloping canopy of pines overhead.

Beyond the silent rows of cottages, a patch of sand was just barely visible, and beyond that a mirror-like reflective sheen that could only be the pond. Emma could just imagine that the rickety old rowboats draped with faded lifejackets still lined the shore, and that if she were to walk down to the water's edge, she would be able to hear the subtle croak of the bullfrogs from the cove on the opposite shore. She smiled at the sense of calm that settled over her as she took it all in.

Just then a sleek, black Mercedes pulled into the driveway behind Emma's car and tooted its horn. From behind the tinted windshield, Emma could just make out the car's sole occupant as he waved cheerfully.

"Hello, hello!" Ted Parker exclaimed, as he jumped out and bustled officiously toward Emma. "So sorry to be a bit tardy, but you know how it is...busy, busy, busy all the time!"

Judging by the worn sheen of his dark suit and the somewhat yellowed, yet nonetheless crisply starched shirt he wore underneath, Emma was not convinced that Ted was really as busy as he claimed...at least with the dubious nature of his so-called real estate business. Before heading for Standish Village, in fact, Emma had taken a detour past the offices of "Parker Realty," and was not exactly impressed. In the first place, the sign identifying the business was of much the same vintage as that of Standish Village, and hung precariously between that of the other two occupants of the tiny plaza in which Ted's office appeared to be located: the "Old Time Chatham Laundromat" and "Hu

Phon Yu's Authentic Canton Dining." Also, despite the fact that it was the middle of the day on a Friday, the parking lot was empty.

"I work mostly from home," Ted Parker told Emma when they talked on the phone several nights earlier. "All this new technology makes commuting to the office every day completely unnecessary."

Not only did Emma doubt that Ted Parker was in possession of any new technology, but she rather suspected that the office of this alleged commute had not been occupied for a number of years. Nonetheless, the longer they talked as the moon slowly rose outside her kitchen window, the more Emma felt a distinct connection between this odd fellow and her fond memories of the Cape. It was as if he understood what it was about this piece of property that enticed her.

"The prime properties are on the water, of course," he told her over the phone, "and by water, I mean the ocean, naturally, but I must confess that I am more fond of the pond real estate."

"Granted there's a significantly smaller commission for agents like me," he added, "but I guess I feel like there is more satisfaction in the tranquility one finds in this kind of sale. You know, where you and the client can stand in the hidden oasis of lily pads and still blue water, distant from the more popular waves, that makes one feel like there might be greater happiness to come."

You're kidding right? Emma thought as she let the phone dangle from her hand in silence. That was a slimy sales pitch if she ever heard one.

"Hello?" Ted Parker inquired tentatively. "Emma, are you still there?"

"Yes, yes, of course," Emma replied hastily, as she pulled the receiver back to her ear.

"And I totally agree…" she added, "I mean about the pond and so forth."

"Good, good," Ted Parker said, obviously relieved. "So, shall we meet at the property tomorrow, say two-ish?"

"That sounds perfect," Emma told him, and hung up.

So here we are, Emma thought as she and Ted Parker stood together at the top of the Standish Village driveway; but now that she was actually standing there, Emma was struck with the sudden reality of the situation. Granted the skeptical look on her teenage son's face earlier may have had a lot to do with her abrupt misgivings, but for a brief moment, Emma felt she might just jump in the car and speed away. As if sensing this, Ted Parker suddenly turned and strode decisively down the hill toward the cottages.

"You coming?" he called over his shoulder. "We've got a lot to see and we're burning daylight!"

Reluctantly, Emma followed.

It quickly became clear that Standish Village had been deserted for more than just the winter months, but Emma tried not to think about what that meant in terms of repairs and renovations. There were the usual tears in the porch screens that Emma remembered her father patiently patching every summer, and a thick blanket of pine needles encased the cottage roofs and porch steps. The lines on the cement shuffleboard court were also in major need of repainting, and the door of the little shed that held the croquet mallets and other lawn game equipment hung precariously by one hinge. The rowboats, too, while lined up side by side on the shore as always, were not especially convincing in terms of their seaworthiness…or was that pond-worthiness? Whatever…cautiously Emma wiggled one of them back and forth in the sand, and shook her head. Damn, she thought, do these things even float?'

Overall, though, Emma was actually more reassured by the condition of the place than she expected to be. The cottages, though empty, had been solidly built and even in the Chatham sea air showed no signs of rot or other forms of deterioration. Granted they could all use a coat of paint, but this was a comparatively minor expense when considering the potential cost of structural repair. And the fact there was very little landscaping to begin with, made sprucing up the few grassy areas and scattered flower gardens seem easily within Emma's maintenance purview.

"I will have to buy all sorts of furnishings," she said tentatively, when Ted Parker's sales approach neared the predictable monetary discussion.

"You will?" he asked. "I guess you might want to do that, but if I were you, I'd just start with the furniture that's in storage."

"In storage?" Emma turned to face the agent. At the time she had been examining the wrought iron number on a cottage she was positive had been the one her family rented in the 70s, but she knew that had been number 9 and currently a "6" hung on the panel next to the door.

"Yes," Ted Parker replied patiently, "just as it says in the listing...cottage furniture has been stored for safe-keeping until the time of the sale."

Though he wasn't reading from a printed listing, he made it sound as though he was. Emma wondered briefly if Ted Parker had memorized all his current listings, but decided it would be rude to ask. Besides, it would also mean she would have to confess she had not read any of them, much less this one. Rather, she would have to admit that she had simply heard about the place being for sale from an old friend whose specific claim to fame was, that at 38, he might still have the same summer job he had when he was 16.

"Oh yes, what's in storage," Emma said quickly. "Of course, I would need to take a look at all that first...to make sure it's suitable, that is."

"Oh, I assure you it's in good repair," Ted Parker remarked confidently. "You see, the past owner was the original owner's grandson, and only owned the place for just over a year."

"Really?" Emma said. She didn't want to add that Standish Village appeared to have been neglected far longer than that.

"Yes, yes," the agent went on. "The fellow had gone off to one of those fancy business schools and when his grandparents passed away, he came back home with all these grandiose plans of making his fortune right here. Had the idea he could transform these little cottages into upscale condo units."

'*These* cottages?" Emma asked. Then fearing that she had been rude, turned toward the door of Cottage #6 and began flipping the number back and forth from the single remaining screw holding it in place. Ah, Emma suddenly realized, the number 9 upside down has become a "6"...of course! It was this revelation that suddenly made her feel as if all of Standish Village was just a little bit off, and, in fact, if looked at in just a slightly different way, that would be just fine.

"What happened?" she asked, turning her attention back to the real estate agent still standing expectantly in the pine needle carpet next to her family's old cottage.

"To the grandson and his plans, I mean," she added quickly, mostly in an effort to cover her recent embarrassment.

Ted Parker shuffled his polished penny loafers nervously and then sighed dramatically.

"It was so sad, really," he said. "Terrible, even. He was so young, you know."

Emma waited patiently for him to continue.

"There was a boating accident, you see," he said at last. "Barely a year after he took over the place. Had it all fixed up and everything, the units were all ready to sell and buyers virtually flocking to the showings!"

"That is sad," Emma agreed, although she actually thought it was more sad that the grandson had turned these perfect, quaint little cottages into condos, but it didn't seem like an appropriate time to mention this.

"It was all so sudden," Ted Parker went on, as if he hadn't heard her. "One day he was building his fortune and the next...well...he was gone."

"Very tragic," Emma said, trying her best to summon up the seemingly required sympathy. "How long ago was this?"

"Hmmm..." Ted Parker replied, rubbing his chin thoughtfully, "Let's see, back in the 90s? Eight, ten years maybe?"

"Eight or ten years!" Emma exclaimed. "And the property has been just sitting here deserted all this time?!"

"Well not deserted, actually..." the agent said hastily, "there's always probate and such...you know, lots that has to happen legally, before anything...well, any real estate transactions can occur."

"But it's been...cared for, the whole time, I assure you," he added.

An awkward silence followed, during which the two of them stood there uncomfortably gazing at the empty village. By this time, the sun was starting to ease its way behind the hearty scrub pines, and in the distance, a fog horn sounded. Overhead, a misguided seagull swooped toward the pond, then perhaps reconsidering its limited food possibilities, nosily flapped away toward the beach.

"Sorry," Emma said at last." I didn't mean to imply that..."

Ted Parker shook his head and waved his hand carelessly.

"No problem," he said, "I can understand your concern. Listen, why don't you come down to the storage place tomorrow and look over what's there by way of furnishings, and if you want, I can even have a quick inspection done of the property...at my expense, of course, just to reassure you everything is in order."

"Thanks," Emma said, somewhat apologetically, "that would be great."

Later at dinner, Luke carefully laid his fork and knife at the edge of his plate and stared silently across the table at his mother. Emma had been chattering nervously while they ordered and ate, offering a stream of reminisces of her childhood on the Cape, and seemed to have barely noticed her son's lack of enthusiastic response. But now, under his studious gaze, she too, lowered her fork and smiled sheepishly in his direction.

"I guess I might be the tiniest bit sentimental about this place," she said.

"You think?" Luke replied. "I mean, seriously, Mom, I know nothing about property values, but from what you told me, this place

69

has been sitting empty for years, plus the guy died in a *boating accident,* for Christ's sake! Sounds to me like he was just a rich kid loser who had no idea what he was doing...not to mention it all sounds a little spooky, like the place might even be haunted or something."

"Don't be ridiculous!" Emma scoffed, though to be honest, the thought had briefly crossed her mind before she hastily brushed it aside.

"Besides, I don't see what all that has to do with me...with us..." Emma pouted nervously, as she absently picked at the few soggy carrots left on her plate.

"As in you...we... actually knowing something about buying and running a place like this?" Luke retorted. "And possibly a haunted one at that. I mean, seriously, don't you kind of wonder why it's been sitting there empty all this time? Why no one bought the place in, what'd that guy tell you, ten years?"

"Eight or ten," Emma said.

Luke sighed and leaned his elbows on the table next to his plate.

Emma grinned.

"I'm sure we can handle it. How hard could it be?" she said, then pushing her plate to one side, she added, "want some dessert?"

"Sure," Luke replied and smiled back. "Why not?"

Chapter Ten: Summer Jobs (1985)

Following Anna's wedding, Emma didn't see Skip again until after her sophomore year at college, where she'd spent two fairly undistinguished years trying to plot some sort of realistic course for her future. By now, her brother, Stephen, at 25, was living in New York City working (he informed his sister) as "the assistant to the assistant of the assistant curator" at the Museum of Modern Art, a job he claimed consisted largely of filing invoices and delivering coffee. Prior to securing this employment, he had managed to acquire several advanced degrees, which, he told Emma, at least gave him something to put on the walls of his tiny fourth floor Brooklyn walk-up.

Emma's oldest brother, Joel, had become, at this point, the manager of the country club at which he had once manicured the greens, for which, in Stephen's words, he drew a salary with at least three more digits than his. Emma did not see either of her siblings as possible role models for her potential life plan.

Thus, when that summer rolled around and two of Emma's college friends proposed heading to the Cape to look for summer jobs, Emma thought, hey, why not?

"Why don't you look up the Petersons?" Emma's father suggested. "They still have their house out there and I'm sure they might have some connections for you and your friends to find some summer work."

Emma knew for a fact that both of the other girls had received considerable scrutiny from their parents regarding the prospect of this summer adventure, and was therefore somewhat taken aback by her father's enthusiasm for the idea. While it occurred to her briefly that her parents had looked forward to a childfree summer (as even Joel had now moved out on his own), she soon realized that considerable communication had already taken place between them and Skip's parents. This was later confirmed when Emma's mother happened to mention that Skip "was so looking forward to seeing" Emma again.

"I can't believe my Mom is still trying to fix me up with some guy I was friends with when I was a little kid!" Emma complained to her friend, Jen.

"Honestly Emma," Jen said, "I really don't think that's such a big deal. I mean if the guy's parents live on the Cape, maybe he's got friends that live there too, and that would make it even more fun to spend the summer out there."

At the time, Jen had her head in Emma's dorm room closet and was casually rifling through her wardrobe.

"You gonna wear this tonight?" she asked as she yanked a striped shirt free from the tangle of hangers and held it up in the air.

"And if not, can I borrow it?" Jen added.

"Yeah, sure," Emma replied. "Borrow anything you want."

Then she sank down on her bed and sighed.

"I just hope Skip's not still hanging out with Caitlin with a C," she said.

"Who?" Jen asked, holding up the shirt as she turned from side to side in front of the mirror.

"Long story," Emma replied.

"This is just so my color!" Jen exclaimed.

Emma realized right then it was going to be a long summer.

As it turned out, by the time Emma and Jen, and their other friend, Amy, arrived on the Cape at the end of the spring semester, Mr. Peterson had already lined up waitressing jobs for all three of them at the Chatham Pub, a small restaurant on Main Street owned and operated by a motherly type, middle-aged woman who called all her female staff "my girls," and flirted shamelessly with the restaurant's young bartender. Her husband, Mac, who was also the chef, was a gruff, bearded, and rather rotund man who barked commands at the kitchen staff, and moved the waitresses' orders to the front based on how often they smiled and winked in his direction.

The Petersons also rented the girls the upstairs of what they called their "carriage house" (which, Emma told Stephen on the phone, was "basically a garage") for a more than reasonable rent. The apartment consisted of one large room divided into a bedroom furnished with three army cots, and a living room/kitchen (if you considered the tiny frig, two-burner stove, and miniature sink a "kitchen"), plus a bathroom in which the shower was barely large enough to turn around. But the three girls loved it for the independence it gave them...not to mention the "leftovers" Mrs. Peterson kept leaving in the fridge, the old stereo and pile of albums that sat in one corner, and the extra cash they could then spend on exploring the other aspects of a college kid Cape Cod summer. And, Emma was startled to realize soon after the three of them had lugged their belongings up the steep set of stairs, it was only a few feet from where Skip lived in the summer.

He was still away at school when the girls moved in, of course, which at first Emma attributed to some romantic relationship Skip was reluctant to abandon. But eventually, Mrs. Peterson let it drop that Skip had "a few courses to make up" and would be staying "down there" for the summer term instead of coming to the Cape right away. The fact that Emma had no idea where "down there" was made her realize that she had lost touch with Skip quite a bit longer ago than she assumed. It was just as well, she decided, since this was supposed to be her "summer adventure" (even though her parents had negotiated the living arrangements), and she didn't need it complicated by some nebulous relationship with a boy she barely knew anymore.

"What did you say this kid's name was?" Amy asked one evening a week or so after they arrived. At the time they were drinking wine purchased at a rather shady convenience store using Jen's fake ID.

"What kid?" Emma replied casually (or at least she thought it was casually).

"The one whose parents rented us our place," Amy said. "You know, the one you used to write letters to...your, whaddya call it? Pen pal?"

"Oh him," Emma said, taking a swig of wine directly from the bottle. "Skip, his name is Skip."

"What kind of a name is that?" Jen asked, as she leaned back drunkenly and gazed up at the slowly fading daylight in the sky above her.

Emma shrugged.

"I don't know," she said. "Something to do with being named after his father and skipping the confusion that caused...I forget."

She didn't really forget, if the truth be known. In fact, she very specifically remembered Skip telling her the whole long story, back when they were 10 years old and sharing a towel on the sandy shore of White Pond. At the time, of course, it seemed very important to her that she understand the source of his nickname, just as it seemed very important to him to be explaining it to her.

"Do you mind being named after someone else?" she remembered asking him. "I mean, not having your own name that's all yours?"

"Well," Skip had answered, "I'm okay with it as long as you think of me as me...that to you, I'm just Skip and not anyone else."

"Of course, I do," Emma had told him. "Why wouldn't I? You're my best friend, after all."

Then, turning toward her with a serious expression, Skip had replied, "and you're mine."

Then he added, even more seriously, "and you always will be."

Just thinking about that conversation that evening with her college friends on the Cape, made Emma sad, somehow. Had she lost something important along the way, she wondered, as she and her friends drank wine and laughed together in the cool breeze of that summer evening on Cape Cod.

Later that night, when the girls were getting ready for bed, Amy pulled one of the old albums from the bottom of the pile on the floor and studied it carefully. The stereo cabinet, though old and worn, contained a well-maintained turntable that had, as one of its useful features, one of those posts on which a number of records could be stacked, and then held in place by a device which allowed them to drop individually onto the turntable itself. After this, the arm holding the player's needle would then automatically swing across, drop down on the selected record and begin to play it. The best part of this was that one could put a pile of favorite albums in place, then slip into bed and peacefully drop off to sleep while the music surrounded you, since the other great feature was automatic shutoff.

"Who's Patti Page?" Amy asked, holding up the album in her hand.

"Who's who?" Jen demanded as she pulled back her covers, punched her pillow a few times, then sat on the edge of her cot.

"Patti Page," Amy replied, turning the battered album over and scrutinizing the print on the cover. "It's a record I found at the bottom of the pile."

"Damned if I know," Jen replied yawning. "Just put the Fleetwood Mac albums on, will ya, so we can get some sleep."

"Featuring her hit song, 'Old Cape Cod'," Amy read from the cover she still held in her hand.

"And there's a humongous picture of her head with, like, some 50s hairdo," she added. "See?"

Amy held up the cover in the direction of her roommates.

"Oh, for God's sake, Ames," Jen groaned, "I'm trying to sleep here. Emma, go put on some real music."

Emma, who had just been dozing off herself, sighed and rolled over.

"What are you guys arguing about?" she demanded, raising herself up on one elbow and rubbing her eyes sleepily.

"Amy found some lame 50s album and wants to play it," Jen explained. "Patti something...has some song called Cape Cod on it."

"Old Cape Cod," Amy corrected her, "and how do you know it's lame if you haven't even heard it. Don't make such a big deal, I'll put it back and find something else."

"No wait!" Emma exclaimed, fully awake now, "Lemme see that!"

Tossing off her covers, Emma swung her legs over the side of the cot, rushed across the room to where Amy stood, and grabbed the album in question out of Amy's hand.

"Geez..." Amy said, "chill, girl."

"Sorry," Emma said, and smiled sheepishly. "It's just that I've been looking all over for this...I mean, I *was* looking all over for it...when I first heard about it...back when I was a kid."

Both of her roommates eyed her cautiously.

"How come?" Amy asked at last.

Emma went back to her cot and sat down, still holding the album.

"It's silly," she said. "Kind of a long story."

"So?" Jen said, as she sat up and leaned her elbows on her knees. "Not like we don't have the time...apart from those bottles of wine we just totaled out back, we don't exactly have a big social life to attend to."

Amy nodded.

"Yeah," she said, "what's with you and Patti and Old Cape Cod?"

"It's stupid really," Emma sighed as she sat back down on the edge of her cot, still holding the album in her hand. "You remember Skip? The guy whose parents are renting us this place?"

The other girls nodded.

"Well, when we were little kids, after we met on Cape Cod, we decided to be pen pals like I told you," Emma explained, "and one time he wrote me this thing about missing 'old Cape Cod'…and something about a 'lobster stew, by a window with a view,' …like putting it in quotes and everything."

"So, I asked my parents why he'd do that…put that in quotes, I mean…" Emma went on, "and they told me it was from a song by Patti Page."

"I looked all over to try and find that record," she added, "and here it is!"

"That's probably why he wrote that to you," Amy said, "because he thought you knew the song and he was trying to tell you something with the lyrics! That's actually pretty romantic!"

"Oh god no, Ames," Emma groaned, as she lay back down on her cot and pulled up the covers. "We were just little kids! He was probably just thinking he was cool because he could quote song lyrics."

"Well," Amy declared, as she picked up the album from where Emma had placed it on the end of her cot, "I want to hear it and see for myself."

"Seriously?" Jen complained.

"Yes," Amy said, and removing the record from its cover, she dropped it onto the turntable and placed the needle on the edge.

"Well put Fleetwood Mac on next, at least," Jen said, as she rolled over to face the wall.

"Will do," Amy replied cheerfully, as Patti Page began to sing.

Emma leaned back and closed her eyes as the words of the song flowed over her.

"If you're fond of sand dunes and salty air
Quaint little villages here and there
You're sure to fall in love with old Cape Cod..."

Slowly Emma slipped back in time to that last evening on the beach with Skip...how the two of them, mere teenagers at the time, sat in the sand planning their futures while in the background the wedding music and laughing voices drifted softly through the night air to where they shared that moment.

"If you spend an evening you'll want to stay, watching the moonlight on Cape Cod Bay," Patti Page crooned as Emma began to doze off. Maybe tomorrow after her shift, she'd hunt up the Petersons and find out exactly when Skip planned to be on the Cape. It'd be nice to see him again, she thought, as she snuggled down further into her covers and fell asleep.

Several days later, Emma found herself still humming that song as she filled the coffee maker at the far end of the bar in the Chatham Pub. It was the middle of the breakfast rush and with most of the tables full, a few hungry customers now overflowed to the bar stools more often occupied by nighttime patrons.

"Hey Miss!" a man called from the end of the bar, "can I get some service here?"

"Be with you in a minute," Emma called over her shoulder. Why was it so difficult to put this coffee pot back together, she wondered, not for the first time, as cursing silently under her breath, she shoved the coffee filter into place. From somewhere within the appliance, came a metallic snap, but nonetheless a brown stream of liquid began to flow through the filter and into the pot below.

"Aarrgghh..." came the voice again, this time in a decidedly pirate-like drawl, "what's a fella gotta do to git some grog!"

"Oh, hold your horses," Emma retorted. Satisfied that despite the noise coming from within the machine, coffee was indeed being produced, she turned to confront the apparently irate customer.

"We don't serve booze this time of day anyhow, so..." she began and then suddenly stopped. At the end of the bar, grinning mischievously in her direction, sat Skip Peterson.

"Oh my God, Skip!" Emma cried, as she hastily wiped her hands on her apron and rushing around the end of the bar, she threw her arms around his neck. "It's so great to see you!"

Though it had been five years since she last laid eyes on her friend, Emma would have recognized him anywhere. Okay, his crazy red curls were somewhat shorter and more contained, and his teenage tees and cutoffs had given way to a starched striped shirt and freshly ironed khaki pants, but the blanket of freckles across his nose and those bright blue eyes still belonged to the little boy she once knew as her best friend.

"Great to see you too, Emma," Skip said, as he gently untangled himself from her embrace. "But don't look now...I think you're getting the evil eye from Mac."

While he played the jolly proprietor around his customers, Mac nonetheless ran a tight ship with his employees.

"When did you get here?" Emma asked as she quickly lowered her voice and slid onto the bar stool next to him.

"Last night," Skip told her. "But it was pretty late, and Mom didn't want me to wake you and your friends."

"Of course, I had to sleep in one of those frilly guest rooms in the main house," he added, "since it seems that some group of wild college girls has taken over my carriage house retreat."

"That's your apartment?" Emma asked. "Oh god, I'm so sorry, your parents never said a word...they just told us to move in."

The door to the kitchen behind them swung open, and a scruffy looking man in a food splattered apron leaned around the edge.

"Hey Emma," he said, "these burgers ain't gonna serve themselves, ya know. I got three or four orders backed up here gettin' cold."

Emma sighed.

"Okay, okay, I'm coming," she said, as she slid off the bar stool.

"Sorry," she told Skip, "I gotta go. See ya later?"

"Sure thing," Skip said.

"My shift ends at four," Emma called over her shoulder as she headed for the pick-up window.

"Meet me at the dock around 6," Skip replied. "We can take the boat out."

Emma turned to ask him what dock (or for that matter, what boat), but by that time, Skip had already left the pub. Oh well, she thought, I'll figure that out later, and she went back to work.

"That guy David called," Amy said, when Emma arrived back at the apartment shortly after five that evening.

"David?" Emma asked. "When? And how did he even get this number?"

Amy shrugged.

"I'm guessing he called your house and maybe your Mom gave it to him?" she said. "Really, Emma, how should I know? Do I look like your personal assistant?"

"Sorry," Emma said. "I'm just sort of surprised he called, that's all."

Amy looked up from the book she was reading.

"You are?" she asked. "I mean back at school, I thought you two were more or less a permanent item. I sort of thought he'd show up sooner or later, but then when you didn't say anything, I figured maybe you wanted to get settled first or something."

"Yeah...or something," Emma replied, as she sank down on her cot.

"The thing is," she said, "I actually asked him if he wanted to come out here...I mean, I invited him to the Cape, and he just said he couldn't commit to anything right then."

"Right when?" Amy said, as she closed her book and studied Emma carefully.

"Before I left school," Emma explained, "you know, a few weeks ago."

"And you haven't talked to him since?" Amy asked.

"No," Emma sighed.

"Haven't talked to who?" Jen demanded, as she climbed the stairs and entered the apartment.

"David," Amy told her.

"Who?" Jen asked. She dropped her keys on the counter and opening the small refrigerator, peered inside hopefully. "Do we have anything to eat?"

"David," Amy repeated. "You know, the guy Emma's been dating back at school."

"He called her today," she repeated helpfully.

"Oh yeah?" Jen said, as she pulled a Tupperware container out of the refrigerator, opened it and examined the contents.

"What is this stuff?" she said, sniffing it suspiciously. Then she put the cover back on, placed it back on the shelf, and closed the refrigerator door.

"Do you guys want to go get some food?" she asked turning to look at her friends.

"I kind of have some place to go," Emma told her, "but you two go ahead."

"Where?" Amy demanded, "and why aren't we going too?"

"Remember my friend, Skip?" Emma said casually, as she wandered over to where Jen stood and started opening cupboards. "He came into the Pub today and said he wants to take me out on his boat tonight...you know, to kind of reconnect."

"Why don't we have any food?" she asked, nonchalantly rummaging through the shelves. Then she turned to look at her friends who stood watching her expectantly.

Jen snickered slightly.

"Oh, come on," Emma said, "Skip and I have been friends since we were nine years-old!"

"Uh, huh...okay, sure..." Amy said grinning. "And what about David?"

"What about him?" Emma said, and smiled innocently.

Erni Johnson

Chapter Eleven: Stored Away (2003)

The morning after her tour of Standish Village with Ted Parker, Emma left the inn early and drove to the storage facility. "I'm off to check out the so-called furnishings," she wrote on the note pad next to the phone. "I'll be back in time for lunch...and maybe a walk on the beach?" Even though her deliberate attempt to sound casual still seemed a little forced, Emma felt certain that Luke would be okay with the note she left him. Besides, she thought, as she glanced over at where he lay sprawled across the hideabed in a tangle of sheets and blankets, he probably wouldn't even wake up before she got back anyhow.

Gathering her purse and windbreaker, she slipped the Do Not Disturb sign over the door knob and quietly left the hotel room, closing the door gently behind her with a reassuring click. Emma was not exactly sure what made her decide to go alone to the facility where the Standish Village furniture was stored instead of bringing Luke along. She tried to tell herself it was because she wanted Luke to have some more vacation time; yesterday he was bursting with excitement over the pictures he'd taken, and impatient to take more today, so it was a logical decision in that respect. Secretly though, Emma also feared that her son's apparent skepticism regarding this whole venture might have some merit, something she really didn't want to consider right now.

It had also crossed her mind that if there was enough time...only if there was enough time, she told herself firmly...she might just go down to the harbor and find out if Skip was working there again. He had been a little vague in his Christmas letter...something about maybe moving back to the Northeast to be closer to his parents? Maybe checking out his old summer job at the Cape? It actually sounded like the marine research work he'd been involved in all these years was beginning to wear on him, and she even sensed what might be some sentimental yearnings between the lines of what he wrote. Well, she could certainly relate to that; after all, the whole reason she was here on the Cape in the first place was to chase down some crazy notion she had about buying Standish Village. Talk about sentimental yearnings!

Oddly, now that Emma thought about it, it seemed like the main point of Skip's Christmas letter this year was to tell her about Standish Village being for sale. The thing is, if it had been on the market for eight or ten years, then why was he just writing her about it now? She probably should have contacted him before coming out here to check things out, but after losing her father and then learning she and Luke would have to find a new place to live, everything just got so complicated, well, that communication simply got lost in the shuffle. Plus, she wasn't even really sure how he'd feel about suddenly hearing from her. How long had it been now? Ten years?

Well, it's not exactly my fault, Emma told herself. I mean, what was she supposed to do? Send letters to his parents' house and hope they would get forwarded? How weird would that be? Besides, even her father had admitted he'd lost touch with their old friends after her Mom died. Emma wasn't even sure that the Petersons lived in New Jersey anymore, much less still came to the Cape in the summer. If only she'd apologized to Skip right after the whole thing happened that summer, back when they were in college, instead of being all stubborn about it. Or if she'd just called him after Stephen arranged that "accidental" meeting in Florida. Both of those things seemed so stupid, now, Emma thought, as she drove into the storage facility parking lot, certainly compared to where life had taken her since.

The storage place appeared deserted when Emma stepped out of her car, and checked her watch. It seemed like Ted Parker would have been here by now, she thought, but maybe he was just running a little late...or at the very least, trying to make her think he was. Busy, busy, busy, she mused, chuckling to herself as she did.

"You Emma?" came a voice from behind her.

Startled, Emma spun around and found herself face to face with an older, white-haired woman who had some of the most intense blue eyes she had ever seen. Interestingly, the woman wore a food-stained white apron over her jeans and flannel shirt, and what appeared to be a hairnet covered her unruly curls, an outfit that quite frankly, seemed out of place in her current surroundings.

"I'm Alice," the woman said, without waiting for Emma to respond. "Ted said you'd be comin' by to take a look at the furnishin's."

"Oh, yes," Emma said, recovering quickly. "He told me he'd be meeting me here. Has he arrived yet?"

She leaned slightly to one side in order to peer around the amply sized woman, hoping for a glimpse of Ted's black Mercedes.

"Nope," Alice said, "he can't make it. Asked me to show you instead."

And with that she turned and walked away.

"Ya comin'?" she called over her shoulder.

"Of course...yes...sure," Emma said, as she hurried after her.

Alice stopped abruptly in front of a nondescript storage unit in the middle of a long row of identical steel doors. She studied it briefly, then produced an enormous set of keys from somewhere within the folds of her apron.

"This here's the one," she said, as she chose one of the seemingly identical keys, and inserted it in the padlock securing the unit. Then with a triumphant grunt (as well as a burst of strength that seemed impossible to Emma based on the woman's evident age), Alice threw open the garage-like door.

"There ya go," Alice remarked, and wiping her hands on her apron, she turned to leave.

"I be back in a bit," she added, nodding briefly in the direction of the storage area. "Take yer time...there's a lot to look through. Meanwhile I got some pies in the oven need tendin' to."

"Um...okay...thanks..." Emma said. "Where will you be if..."

But the woman had already disappeared around the corner of the building.

It struck Emma that she hadn't noticed any sort of a house on the property when she drove in, but it was possible Alice lived somewhere nearby, she supposed. Still, it seemed a bit strange that the woman would be making pies (plural, no less) at this time of day in the middle of the week. Ah well, probably one of those locals who sold baked goods out of her kitchen, Emma thought. She made a mental note to check it out before she left...it'd be nice for Luke to experience an old-fashioned, homemade Cape Cod pie. It might even make him a bit less cynical about this whole venture...what was it her father used to say about her brothers? The way to a teenage boy's heart is through his stomach? Something like that.

The storage unit was windowless, dark, and chilly, but just to the left of the open door, Emma discovered a light switch and flipped it to the on position. Overhead, a single bulb, dangling from the high ceiling illuminated the area in which she stood. The room itself proved to be quite a bit larger than it appeared on the outside, and rather than the chaotic jumble of furnishings she had expected, Emma found herself surrounded by a collection of neatly stacked and organized items, each grouping labelled with a number...presumably identifying the cottage to which it belonged. White wooden headboards leaned heavily against the walls, held firmly in place by matching bureaus, and end tables, each topped with an array of different size lamps in various seaside motifs.

Everything had been meticulously covered with crisp white drop cloths, the edges of which Emma lifted carefully as she peered underneath. There was a uniformity to the selection of furnishings, much as Emma had expected; if, in fact, the grandson had planned to sell the cottages as condos, the new owners would certainly be adding their own personal touches.

Emma had pretty much finished her perusal of the contents of the unit when she noticed a less uniform group of furniture on the far wall. It, too, was covered by a drop cloth, but this one was a light shade of blue, rather than the stark white of the others. She lifted the edge of the blue cloth and peered underneath; there sat a miniature dresser with a small seashell lamp balancing precariously on top.

"Found that in Cottage 9," came a voice from behind her. "Cute little thing ain't it? It was kinda stuffed back in a little storage area...don't think anyone saw it when we was first cleanin' things out, so I just brung it along with the rest."

Emma guiltily released the drop cloth, turned slowly around and was face to face once more with Alice. This time, though, Alice had abandoned the apron in favor of a worn gray sweater now covering the rest of her original outfit. Gone as well was the hairnet, and the previously trapped white curls now softly framed her face as, for the first time, Emma realized, the woman smiled.

"Adorable!" Emma exclaimed, unwilling for some reason to reveal that she had seem the bureau and its lamp many times before. "Perhaps intended for a child's room?"

Alice studied her carefully.

"I imagine so," she said at last. "I used to clean them cottages when they belonged to the older Andersons back in the 70s...a lotta families stayed there in those days as I recall."

"It seems like a it would be a nice family place," Emma remarked, turning back to the storage unit in order to prevent Alice from seeing her expression. Although she'd been quick to let Charlie at the bandstand know of her childhood connection with the Cape, she had since wondered if she might have said too much. This was coastal New England, after all, and the reluctance with which the residents welcomed "summer people" into their everyday lives was well-documented among the travel writers.

"Is this all the furniture?" Emma asked, waving her hand in the general direction of the unit's contents.

"Oh lordy, no," Alice replied, chuckling to herself. "There's three or four more units just like this 'un, but Ted, he said to just show youse a sample so you could git the gist. Didja want me to open the others?"

"Oh no," Emma replied hastily, "I get the picture. I'm just impressed that it all looks...so new."

Alice gazed quizzically at Emma and cocked her head slightly.

"Didn't Ted tell you about young Gordy and what happened and all?" she asked.

"No...wait, yes... the guy with the boat accident and the condos, you mean?" Emma said.

"Right," Alice told her. "Gordy Anderson, the one inherited the place from his grandparents. He's the one bought all this stuff...wholesale, was what he told everyone, brand new!"

Then she shook her head.

"Said he was gonna furnish all the places with this cheap stuff, so people could imagine what they would look like when they put in their own stuff," she explained.

"Seems like a damn waste to me," she added. "But then what do I know?"

"Well," Emma said, as she stepped out of the unit and waited for Alice to close and lock the door, "If I buy Standish Village it won't be to make condos out of it. I just want to make it like it used to be...a friendly place for families to go on their vacations."

"And in that case," she added, "I think this furniture will be just fine."

"Well, bless you dear," Alice said, as she pulled down the door to the unit and reinserted the padlock, "I sure hope it works out for ya. It was just like that in the old days, ya know...back when I used to work over there. I just loved seein' all those kids runnin' around, and families spendin' time together. You just don't see much 'a that anymore."

Emma smiled and nodded in agreement, but Alice didn't seem to notice. The woman just stood there in front of the storage unit, gazing silently at the closed door. Feeling somewhat awkward, Emma turned and started to walk toward her car. Then abruptly she realized she had not thanked Alice for showing her the furniture. But when she turned back to do so, Alice was gone. Oh well, Emma thought, I'll just tell Ted Parker to let her know how much I appreciated her help.

The clock on the dash read 10:15 when Emma climbed back into her jeep. Plenty of time before meeting Luke for lunch, she thought. Maybe I'll just take a drive down to the harbor and look at the boats before I head back to the inn.

Okay, be honest with yourself, girl, she admitted, as she turned the key in the ignition, you know you want to see if Skip's there. And what would be wrong with that? she asked herself. He's just an old friend, not to mention the one who told her about Standish Village being on the market and all. It's the least you could do to see if he's around, and, you know, thank him, despite what happened between them in the past. It was years ago, right? And since he still wrote her letters every so often, he had to be over it, she told herself...she certainly was anyhow. It only took a few minutes to persuade herself this was the right thing to do, and even less time to realize she was already driving in the direction of the harbor.

The docks were pretty quiet when she arrived; it was not quite time for the pre-dawn fishing boats to return and unload their catch, and it was still too early in the season for the wealthy summer crowd to be cruising across to the beach on the other side of the protected area. Consequently, when Emma parked in the nearly deserted lot and hiked down the paved incline toward the water, the only real sounds were the cries of hungry gulls and a distant church bell announcing the half hour somewhere in town.

There was no one in sight as she wandered cautiously across the weather beaten commercial dock, but suddenly a buzzing noise from within one of the ramshackle buildings on the wharf caught her attention. Moving slowly in the direction of the sound, Emma soon reached an open doorway from which it seemed to be emanating. Then, as abruptly as the noise began, it simply stopped.

"Hello?" Emma called into the opening. "Anybody here?"

As her eyes adjusted slowly to the diminished light, she stepped into the shack and came face to face with what at first appeared to be an alien from another planet.

"Oh!" Emma cried as she leaped back. The figure in front of her was dressed in dark coveralls, and grungy rubber boots, his face concealed by a menacing looking plastic shield and a pair of green goggles. In his hand he held a fierce looking weapon of some sort from which protruded what was obviously a mass of sharp metal blades.

"Thought I heard someone out here," the alien said, rather cheerfully, Emma observed, for a space invader. Then the creature removed the face shield and shoved the googles up on top of his perfectly normal human head.

"Hey," the man said, "you okay, Miss? Ya look kinda spooked."

"Um...sorry..." Emma said, as she caught her breath, "I thought you were..."

"Thought I was who?" he said. Setting down the orbital sander, he wiped his hands on his coveralls, ran them through his chaotic black curls in some sort of grooming effort, then reached out to shake Emma's hand.

"Caleb," he said, "Caleb Mitchell...but everyone just calls me Cal."

Emma smiled sheepishly.

"Emma Lakin," she told him as she shook his outstretched hand.

"Phew!" Cal exclaimed, as he sat down on an overturned crate nearby. "You gave me quite a scare! Didn't think anyone was around, and what with all the noise the sander was makin'...well, I didn't hear ya come in."

Emma thought it would be better if she didn't mention her own first impression.

"Sorry," she said. "I was looking for a friend of mine...he used to work here. I mean, I think he might be working here now...that is, again...but I haven't seen him for a while so I don't know if he..."

"What's the fella's name?" Cal interrupted.

"Skip," Emma said, "Skip Peterson."

Cal scratched his head thoughtfully.

"Doesn't ring a bell," he said, "but then I'm pretty new here, so could be he just hasn't been in during one of my shifts. When did you last see him around here?"

"I didn't actually see him here," Emma said, "At least not for a while. Quite a while actually...but I hear from him, you know, letters and stuff, and he talks about it...maybe working here at the harbor... again, that is."

Cal nodded.

"Lotta guys work here," he remarked patiently. "What I'm saying is, could be I just haven't met him yet. You know how it is, guys coming and going all the time, busy workin' on different stuff..."

"Of course," Emma replied quickly. "I understand."

Then she turned to leave.

"If you want, you can write his name down and...and ...yours too, I s'pose, and if I see him, I could maybe tell him you were here?" Cal called after her hopefully.

"That is, if you want..." he added.

Emma turned back and glanced hesitantly in Cal's direction. He seemed like a nice guy and all, but still you never know, Emma thought. It probably wouldn't be a great idea to tell him where she was staying, even though she did want to get a message to Skip. Maybe it'd be better to just stop by Skip's parents' house instead.

"That's okay," she said finally. "I can just come by another time...or you know, give him a call."

Cal shrugged.

"If you say so," he said, and shrugged. Then, picking up the sander once more, he disappeared back into the shack.

"Thanks anyway," Emma called into the darkness, but the only reply was the renewed insistent buzz of Cal's sander. Oh well, she thought, who knows when Skip's next shift was anyhow...she and Luke might be back in Albany by then and besides, the last time she knew for sure Skip worked here had to be back when they were both in their 20s. He was a marine biologist now, for God's sake...why would he go back to working at harbor? Still, he did say the guys at the boatyard told him about Standish Village.

It was all pretty confusing now that Emma thought about it, as she trudged back up the hill to where she'd parked her jeep. If only she'd read his note a little more carefully...or could remember where she left it, for that matter. As she climbed into the driver's seat, a strong sweet odor that seemed, oddly enough, to be coming from the back seat, wafted enticingly through the car. Placing her keys on the dash, she twisted in her seat and peered behind her. There on the seat was a square bakery box.

Reaching over the gear shift, Emma gingerly picked it up and pulled it into the front, where she placed it on her lap. The inviting smell was stronger now...like berries...blueberries maybe, mixed with a sugary baked sweetness that could only be...pie...blueberry pie, Emma realized as she opened the cover of the box and inhaled its welcoming and somehow familiar odor.

Then she remembered: every summer when they came to the Cape, her father would announce he had to go run an errand, and then in a great swirl of feigned secrecy, would hop in the car and disappear. When he returned a short time later, he would be carrying a box, just like the one she now held in her lap, and that same sweet blueberry smell would fill the cottage.

"Life is short," he would always declare, "so eat dessert first!"

And they all would...she, her mother, her father, and her brothers, all sitting together around the old wooden picnic table on the porch of Cottage #9.

But where did this one come from? Emma wondered as she again closed the cover of the box she held in her lap. Then she saw the note.

"Welcome back to Cape Cod!" it said. "Thought you might enjoy this little taste of the coast. Alice."

Chapter Twelve: Sentimental Journey (2003)

"Wow, Mom! This is really good!" Luke exclaimed, as he stuffed an oversized bite of what had recently been designated by both he and his mother as "lunch" into his mouth. They were sitting on the stone wall overlooking the Chatham Light Beach with Alice's blueberry pie balanced between them, and although they had decided to "share," it was obvious from his blue lips and tongue that Luke's portion might have turned out to be a bit larger. Emma didn't care, actually; she was just happy to be there on this unseasonably warm spring day, sharing the view with her son.

"Where did you say you got this again?" he asked between mouthfuls.

"This lady named Alice," Emma told him. "She owns...or maybe just manages...the storage facility where the furniture is stored."

"Actually," she added, "she left it in my car...not sure when...I didn't see her do it, is what I'm saying. She just left a note..."

"Furniture?" Luke said, as he briefly stopped chewing. "What furniture?"

"You know, the furniture from the Standish Village cottages, the stuff that's in storage," Emma said, casually, she hoped. "I told you about that, right?"

Then she picked up her binoculars and trained them on the far end of the beach...it was early in the season, but there still might be seals out there. She couldn't remember what her father used to tell her about the migration patterns...when was it they showed up? Or was that the sharks? Did seals even migrate? She'd have to look that up. It was at that moment she realized Luke had stopped eating and was staring at her intently.

"What?" she said, slowly lowering the binoculars and turning in his direction.

"Nothing," he said, "it's just that...it's just that I was thinking maybe you were done with that."

"Done with what?" Emma demanded. "With the idea of buying Standish Village, you mean? Why would you think that?"

Luke shrugged.

"I don't know," he said. "After you toured the place and stuff...well... it seemed like maybe your expectations weren't quite ...fulfilled? Once you thought it over, I mean."

Emma looked back out toward the water and sighed. A lone fishing boat chugged its way through the ocean inlet toward the harbor docks, nets dangling idly from the hook off its stern. In the wake of the puttering motor, a few curious seagulls floated expectantly, perhaps hoping for a scrap or two of the day's catch.

"I guess I haven't decided yet," Emma said. "I need a little more information, of course, but I also have to think about the whole thing and how it will work. I'd have to finish the school year, naturally, but if I want to open the place this summer, then I'll have to start coming out on weekends to work on it, that is after the sale goes through...if there is a sale...or whatever."

Luke nodded thoughtfully.

"And then what?" he asked. "I mean, we'll just move out here? It's not that I don't think the Cape is cool, Mom, it's just that, you know, there's school and everything, and...well... I'm not sure I want to change...schools, that is."

If Emma was completely honest with herself, she'd have to admit she hadn't thought about that aspect of the whole thing. Was it really fair, in other words, to uproot Luke from all his friends and his life back in Albany...where he was born and had always lived...and drag him out here to live? Based on some notion she suddenly had, to buy Standish Village? Or was it her *need* to buy the place? She was startled by this abrupt thought. Why would she suddenly *need* to buy a cottage colony on Cape Cod?

"Sorry," Luke said, as he picked up the pie box and a bit too purposefully, it seemed to Emma, dug into the contents again. "It's just that..."

Emma reached over and squeezed her son's arm.

"It's fine, Luke," she said. "I want to hear what you think...and how you feel. I won't do anything without talking it all over with you first, Okay? Really."

"I promise we'll decide together," she added. Luke looked up and smiled.

"I gotta say, though," he remarked, "if this pie is going to be a regular item on the lunch menu, then I'm in."

Later, as they drove back to the inn, Emma slowed at a familiar looking intersection, then turned abruptly up a side street and parked in front of a large, white clapboard house. Luke looked up from the map he held in his lap.

"I think you took a wrong turn back there, Mom," he said. "This looks like a dead end."

But Emma wasn't listening. She rolled down her window and was now leaning out and studying the house carefully.

"Mom?" Luke said again.

Emma turned toward her son.

"What?" she replied. "Oh...sorry, Luke. Yes, I know this isn't the way to the inn. I saw that street sign back there and just remembered this is where my friends and I lived one summer when we were in college...you know, the time I told you about, when I came out here to the Cape with Jen and Amy, and we all got summer jobs here in Chatham?"

Luke leaned forward in his seat and peered out through the driver's side window at the large white house.

"You lived *here* in college?" he asked. "Are you sure? No offense, Mom, but this is a pretty huge house for college kids to be able to afford, even if you were just renting."

"Well not exactly here," Emma explained. "We lived behind it. The house belonged to my friend, Skip's parents, and they rented us an apartment upstairs in the carriage house."

"Carriage house?" Luke said. "What's a carriage house?"

"Kinda like a garage," Emma told him.

"A garage!" Luke declared. "You lived in a garage?"

But Emma had already gotten out of the car and was walking up the driveway.

"Where are you going?" Luke said, as he, too, climbed out of the car and hurried after his mother. "You can't just walk onto somebody's property, you know. I mean without asking or anything..."

By the time he caught up with her, Emma was standing at the end of the front walk leading to the house, and leaning slightly to one side in an effort to see around the back of the building.

"Mom!" Luke said again. Emma turned and smiled at him calmly.

"Don't worry, Luke," she said, patting him gently on the shoulder. "I know the people who live here. They were friends with Gramps. They're Skip's parents."

"But Mom," Luke insisted, "what if..."

Just then the front door of the house opened, and out stepped a slim young woman balancing a chubby baby on one hip.

"Can I help you?" she asked, not unkindly.

"Hello...yes," Emma replied cheerfully, "I'm Emma Lakin and this is my son, Luke."

While it occurred to Emma that this might be the youngest of the Peterson sisters, her hair lacked the red curls Emma would have expected, and on closer inspection, the woman seemed quite a bit younger than Emma thought she would be by now. Ah well, people do change their hair color...and some people age better than others, she thought, a bit ungenerously perhaps.

"I'm Kate," the woman said, as she bounced the cherubic baby slightly, then added, "and this is Christopher."

Then she stood waiting rather expectantly.

"I was looking for the Petersons," Emma explained awkwardly, then paused. "This is...was...I mean, used to be...their summer place."

"I think you have the wrong house," Kate said cautiously, as she gestured in the general direction of the neighborhood beyond. "There are a lot of similar homes on this block."

"My husband and I bought this place a few years ago," she added, "from some people named Curtis, I think. I don't know anyone named Peterson."

"Mom," Luke said, tugging on his mother's sleeve, "let's go...this isn't the place you thought it was, and I think we're creeping this lady out."

"No wait," Emma said, freeing her arm from her son's grip, "I know this is the place."

Then she turned to the woman standing at the front door.

"Isn't there a carriage house out back? With an apartment over it?" she asked. "That's where my friends and I lived when we were in college...the summer we came out here to work on the Cape."

Kate frowned briefly, then brightened.

"Why yes," she said, "there is...or at least there was."

"My husband did some research on the house when we moved in, and wanted to renovate," she explained, "you know, so we could do that and wouldn't impact the historical value in the process."

"One of the things my husband discovered was that there used to be a carriage house out back...from when the only transportation was house and buggy, I suppose," she went on. "Then of course, it became a garage later...and the apartment upstairs was designed for the chauffeur apparently."

"But it's not there anymore?" Emma asked. "The carriage house, I mean?"

"Oh no," Kate said, "it burned down back in the mid 90s sometime...before we lived here. We're planning on building a garage back there, but I guess there's some historic significance in regard to the foundation."

She shrugged.

"You know how it is," she said. "The historical society wants to come out and dig up what's left...sift through the remains, so to speak. But of course, they have to wait until their budget allows for it. And who knows when that will be?"

"At least it's not an eyesore," Kate added, "or potentially dangerous for this little guy...when he gets a little older, that is. Apparently, it burned to the ground...nothing left but the rock foundation."

She bounced the now wiggling baby in her arms slightly as she spoke.

"You can go back and take a look if you want..." she said. "I've got to go feed this little guy, so..."

"Thanks," Emma said, "but we...uh...we've got to get going anyhow."

"Okay," Kate remarked cheerfully, "have a nice day."

Then she stepped back inside the house and closed the door.

Emma and Luke walked back to their car in silence.

"Sorry, Mom," Luke said, once they were inside the Jeep. "It must be weird to hear about what happened to that place you rented and all."

Emma sat staring at the house for a minute or two, then turned and smiled at her son.

"No biggie," she said. "I was just thinking that if the Petersons still lived here, maybe I could ask them how to get in touch with their son...my friend, Skip. I kinda thought it might be fun for you to see him again, now that you're older. You know, see if you do remember him after all, and...well...find out what he's up to these days."

Then she smiled brightly again.

Luke nodded, then reached down and picked up the map.

"I guess being out here on the Cape again has brought back a lot of memories for me," Emma said, as she started the car and pulled away from the curb.

"Good memories?" Luke asked.

"Some good," Emma told him, "and some not so good, too."

"Yeah," Luke said, "I get what you mean. Some places feel like that for me also."

I hope not, Emma thought, but rather than tell him this, she just reached over, patted her son's arm and smiled.

"Ice cream?" she suggested.

"Perfect!" he said. "After all that pie, I could really use some dessert."

Chapter Thirteen: Emma and Skip (1985)

By the time Emma reached the dock that long ago summer night she agreed to meet Skip at his boat, it was 6:20; which wasn't too bad, considering she was on foot and had made more than one wrong turn.

"It's about time!" Skip exclaimed, as he reached up from the deck of his boat to help her aboard. "I was thinking maybe you stood me up."

"Well, it might have helped if you told me which dock," Emma grumbled as she attempted to step into the boat gracefully, something that was clearly not destined to happen.

Skip gripped her hand tightly and eased her on to the deck. Then he grinned mischievously.

"Like there's more than one boat dock in Chatham," he said. "And since you basically live at my house, I know for a fact it's less than a five minute drive from there."

"Yeah," Emma retorted, "if you have a car that is."

"You're working on the Cape all summer and you don't have a car?" Skip exclaimed. "How are you getting around?"

Emma sat down on one of the cushioned benches lining the stern of the 25-foot Runabout, took off her sneakers and rubbed her feet. Wearing the new ones was not a good plan, she decided, and not for the first time, reprimanded herself for being overly conscious of the evening's chosen wardrobe.

"My friend, Amy, has a car," she explained, "that's how we got to the Cape...and how we get around...but she and my other friend, Jen, went to get something to eat and so I had to walk down here."

Skip observed her silently for a few minutes, then he turned and headed toward the bow.

"Did you consider asking them for a ride before they left?" he called over his shoulder casually.

"And did you consider asking me if you could pick me up," Emma declared, "since, as you so adroitly pointed out, it's less than a five minute drive from where we're *both* living?"

Skip started the boat's engine with an abrupt roar, and looked over his shoulder to where Emma now sat sulking.

"Wanna come sit up front with the Captain, Miss?" he said with mock formality. "Might even let ya take the wheel if ya behave."

Emma scowled, then started to laugh. Sure enough, the same old incorrigible Skip, no matter how many years went by...still her very best friend in all the world, no matter who else came and went in her life. And still impossibly funny, even when she was trying so hard to be serious.

"I reckon I will," she said, and steadying herself against the rail, she made her way to the bow and climbed onto the seat next to his.

"Let 'er rip," she announced.

"Okay," Skip replied, "but it might be a good idea to untie 'er first."

If Emma was to say...okay, admit...what were the best moments of that summer on the Cape after her sophomore year, she would unquestionably choose that evening she and Skip went out on his boat. Of course, she never would have told Amy and Jen that, because it was also true that the weeks they shared on the Cape were some of the best times of Emma's life as well, and more than crucial to cementing their friendship.

But now, almost twenty years later, Emma could remember very few details from the time she spent with her girlfriends, but could still recall nearly every second she spent with Skip that evening ...and of course, sadly, afterwards as well.

"So M'lady," Skip said, once they were underway, "where would you like to go?"

"Mmmm...Let me see..." Emma mused leaning back in her seat. "Portugal perhaps? Or how about some Caribbean island? I've always wanted to do that. And then there's Bermuda."

Skip shook his head.

"Nope," he said, "can't do that, what with the triangle and all. How would I explain that to your parents? Or for that matter, how would anyone explain it to mine?"

"And I'm not sure I have enough gas to get us to Portugal," he added. "How about Pleasant Bay? It's beautiful and calm there this time of day and the view of the moon is outrageous!"

"Oh yeah?" Emma sneered, glancing sideways at him. "And just how is it you know about said outrageous moon? Is that where you take all your lady passengers?"

Skip stared straight ahead and chuckled.

"I shall never divulge my secrets," he said.

"However," he added, without turning his head, "I doubt anything could be as beautiful as 'watching the moonlight on Cape Cod Bay'."

"Oh yeah?" Emma said, "and how would you know about that?"

Skip shrugged.

"Just something I did once with a girl I used to know," he remarked.

"Well," Emma replied smugly, "I guess if you spend the evening you'll want to stay..."

"On old Cape Cod..." Skip said, finishing the lyric. Then he turned to look at Emma as he slowed the boat and glided it gently into Pleasant Bay.

"Found the album, didja?" he said.

Emma nodded.

"Sure did," she said. "Well, actually my roommate, Amy, did, but I remembered it right away...and we listened to it that same night. Are those all your albums up there? In the apartment, I mean?"

"Some belonged to my sisters," Skip said, "but most of them are mine, yeah. To be honest, though, I don't know where that Patti Page record came from. Somebody must have left it at our house or something. But when I was a little kid, for some reason I was really into that song."

"I know," Emma said. "You actually quoted the lyrics to me in a letter once, when you were like 12 or something."

"Seriously, I did?" Skip exclaimed. "God, what a dork I was, huh?"

"Nope," Emma told him, "I didn't think you were a dork at all. In fact, I spent months trying to find that record and never could."

"Okay," Skip teased, "then you're the one that's a dork. That's a relief!"

And with that he cut the motor, climbed back into the stern and dropped the anchor.

"Wine, M' lady?" he asked, opening a cooler strapped to the deck.

"Why certainly," Emma replied, as she slid out of her seat and went to join him.

"Good," Skip said, "let's drink a few glasses and take in some constellations, shall we? Just for old time's sake, of course..."

Emma had never been much for stargazing...mostly because she could never really see any of those formations everyone else was pointing to and somehow making into pictures of goddesses or zodiac signs or whatever...but that night on Skip's boat, as they drank wine and lay back together on the floor of the deck, it was like she could see everything he pointed out with perfect clarity.

Hours later, as they chugged quietly into the harbor, Emma could not figure out where the time had gone. More importantly, as she stepped none too gracefully from the boat deck to the dock, she was not altogether sure how she'd find her way back to the carriage house in the dark. Skip stood staring at the boat he had just secured to the dock.

"I guess I can take this out to the mooring in the morning," he said finally, "that way I can take you home now."

Then he hesitated.

"However...I'm not sure I should be driving...my car I mean..." Skip admitted sheepishly, as he tightened the mooring ropes and joined Emma on the dock.

"Yeah, well," Emma said, "I'm not sure I should be walking either...home, that is."

"Okay," Skip remarked cheerfully, draping his arm over her shoulder, "then how about we just negotiate this walking home thing together."

"Sounds like a plan," Emma agreed, "especially since I assume you know the way."

Skip shrugged.

"We'll soon find out," he said and together they set off on foot.

A short time later, they reached the Peterson's street and headed down the sidewalk toward Skip's house.

"There, ya see?" Skip declared, "I'm a human compass!"

"Amazing," Emma scoffed, "twenty years old and he can actually find his way home...somewhere he's lived every summer for years."

"Yeah, well there is that," Skip said, then he started humming.

"How does that song go anyhow?" he said, "the Old Cape Cod thing, I mean...I haven't heard it in so long, I can't remember."

Emma slowed and began to hum a little herself. Then gave up.

"Something about sand dunes and salty air..." she suggested.

"Oh yeah, yeah," Skip responded eagerly, "and quaint little villages here and there!"

Then he draped his arm across Emma's shoulder again and started to sing: "You're sure to fall in love with old Cape Cod!"

Emma laughed and joined in as they turned into Skip's driveway,

"Cape Cod! That old Cape Cod!" They sang loudly, albeit a bit tunelessly.

Then, abruptly, Emma stopped walking and stood staring at the powder blue VW bug parked at the curb.

"If you like the taste of a lobster stew..." Skip sang on, before realizing he was doing so alone.

"Emma?" he said, "what's wrong?"

But Emma was already moving quickly toward the carriage house, the crushed shells under her feet crunching loudly beneath the stiff soles of her new sneakers. In front of her, at the end of the darkened stretch of driveway, a figure stepped out of the shadows and moved into the glow of the lights coming from the main house.

"David?" Emma said hesitantly, as she moved closer to the young man standing in front of her.

"Of course, it's me," David said, "who did you expect?"

"I...I...just wasn't expecting you," Emma stuttered, "when did you get here?"

David checked his watch.

"Let's see..." he drawled sarcastically, "about three hours ago...an hour or so after I left you a message that I was coming over. With that friend of yours, what's her name? Jess?"

"Jen," Emma said.

"Right, Jen," David replied.

They stood there awkwardly while Emma desperately tried to remember Jen giving her a message. Then it came to her...the phone ringing when she was in the shower before her friends left for dinner, and Jen knocking on the bathroom door.

"Hey Ems," she had shouted over the roar of the running water, "there's a message for you on the counter. That guy called again."

"Okay, okay!" Emma remembered calling back, assuming of course, that it was Skip checking up on her, wondering when she'd be at the boat.

"I'm coming. Geez, it's not even 5:30!" she fumed as she turned off the shower and grabbed her towel from a nearby hook.

And then, naturally, once she realized she was really running late, dashing out of the apartment without bothering to even read the note Jen left behind.

"Where have you been?" David was saying now, "and who's that guy?"

By this time, Skip had caught up with Emma and was now standing next to her catching his breath and staring cautiously at David.

"David, this is my friend, Skip," Emma said. "Skip, this is…David."

Skip smiled cheerfully and extended his hand, which David seemed to ignore. Instead, he stepped forward, wrapped his arm possessively around Emma's waist and pulling her towards him, gave her a clumsy kiss.

"Nice to meet you," he said to Skip over Emma's left shoulder.

"Same," Skip remarked, then turned in the direction of the house.

"Later Emma," he said as he walked away.

"Sure thing," she called after him, then releasing herself from David's embrace, she took his hand and led him down the driveway. When they got to the Carriage House, she sat down on the small wooden bench next to the door to the apartment and pulled him down beside her.

"What are you doing here?" she demanded.

'Hey," David said, "can't a guy come and visit his girl without getting the third degree?"

"Besides," he added, slipping his arm around her again, "you invited me, remember?"

"What I remember," Emma said, removing his arm from her shoulders, "is you telling me you couldn't 'confirm anything right now'."

She punctuated the final statement with air quotes as she shifted and faced him angrily.

David shrugged.

"I missed you," he said, then looked down and began shuffling his feet nervously.

Oh god, Emma thought, do I actually feel sorry for this guy? After all he put me through? Especially since David's inability to "commit" to her Cape invitation was only part of it. For starters, when they first started going out in the fall, he had neglected to mention he still had a girlfriend at home. Okay, fine, lots of college relationships start out that way, and then as time goes by, absence tends to stop making the heart grow fonder, as they say, and the here and now eventually wins out.

She probably should have inquired further about the girlfriend situation somewhere along the way, Emma realized now; at least casually brought up the subject after they'd been together for a while...seriously together, in fact, certainly enough so, that it would have been only natural to discuss the nature of their relationship. Of course, it wasn't like David actually lied to her, he just never mentioned anything more about "Kelly" one way or another after a few months, and the more involved she and David became, the more awkward it would have been for Emma to ask for an update.

"It was so cool you were there for David when Kelly dumped him," one of David's friends, Carl, told Emma one evening after a few too many beers. "he was really broken up about it."

It was early in January at the time, and Emma remembered feeling truly pleased with herself that she'd never said anything more after David admitted having a hometown girlfriend when they first went out back in the fall. It must have been right after we met that they broke up, she concluded that evening when she was drinking with Carl, and even if I was possibly a rebound relationship, she and David had stayed together happily ever since they met. Maybe this girl even dumped him because he told her about me, she thought rather smugly, as she smiled sweetly at her companion.

"I'm glad I was too," she told Carl, generously patting him on the arm.

"Yeah," he went on, taking another swig of his beer, "can you believe, that after he gave her that fancy necklace for Christmas, that she just blew him off? What a bitch!"

Granted, when she finally confronted David a month later (on Valentine's Day, no less) with the actual timing of his break-up with Kelly, he had reached for her hand across the restaurant table and swore it was "over with Kelly way before that," and that he just hadn't "had the heart to tell her," especially not "in person." So naturally he waited until he went home for the Christmas holidays. Certainly, Emma could understand that, right? And, of course, Emma believed him, especially when after she told him what Carl said, David looked truly shocked and exclaimed, "you're kidding, he said that?" then added, "I bet he was just hitting on you for himself."

Plus, at dinner that same night, David had given her a beautiful turquoise necklace as a Valentine's gift. Later, though, Emma stopped wearing it for reasons she could not explain and eventually told David that she let someone in her dorm borrow it and the girl never returned it. She felt a little guilty about lying to him, but something about that necklace had always nagged at her, and once again, as time went by, it seemed as though it might be awkward to ask him where it actually came from originally. The odd thing was, that when Emma told David the necklace was missing, it didn't seem to bother him and he never mentioned it again.

And once again, that summer evening on the bench by the carriage house, David, seemed sincerely contrite.

"It just wasn't the same after you left for the Cape," he was saying, as he reached for Emma's hand. "I was trying to be understanding about letting you have your summer with your friends, and I just figured, you know, I'd hang with mine...give you a little space."

"But oh my god, Emma," he declared squeezing her hand tightly and staring into her eyes, "I just can't believe how lost I am without you!"

Emma stood abruptly and turned away.

"So where are you staying?" she asked quietly.

"One of the guys' parents has a house down here," David said, a bit too cheerfully it seemed to Emma, but she ignored her reaction and just stood there silently.

"It's a big house," he went on. "I mean, if you want, you can come back there with me...you know, hang out together...maybe spend the night?"

Emma took a deep breath and then turned to look at him. In the half light of the moon, David appeared much the same as always ...handsome, endearing, and somehow sweet. Yet at the same time, a stream of not all that comfortable memories from the recent school year they had spent most of together stealthily slid through her mind.

"I have an early shift tomorrow," she lied, as she fumbled for her apartment key.

David said nothing.

"But maybe we can meet up later?" Emma added hastily.

Then he brightened.

"Sounds like a plan," David announced, as he stood up from the bench and gave her a quick hug. Then he turned and crunched his way back down the driveway toward his car, waving cheerfully over his shoulder. Emma smiled and waved back.

"You jerk," she said, as she unlocked the apartment door, but then wasn't sure whether she was referring to David or herself.

Chapter Fourteen: Homeward Bound (2003)

On Monday morning after breakfast, Emma and Luke packed the car and headed for home. Despite his patience with the whole adventure, Emma knew her son was anxious to get back to his life in Albany, and perhaps salvage a bit of his vacation with some of his friends who were still in town.

"Thanks for coming to the Cape with me," Emma said, once they checked out of the inn and were on the road. Luke was leaning forward in his seat, fussing with the radio dial.

"Huh?" he said looking over at Emma. "Oh yeah, sure, no problem. Hey, what's the deal with the radio stations out here? I can't find anything that remotely resembles music."

Emma glanced over at the dial Luke was carelessly spinning back and forth.

"Yeah, well," she admitted, "you might not find much until we get on the highway...the highway on the other side of the bridge, that is."

"Seriously?" Luke demanded. "I thought you spent the whole summer out here when you were in college! What did you do? For tunes, I mean?"

"Oh, we had some records," Emma said.

"You know, albums?" she added. "Stuff we used to play in the apartment before we went to sleep. And then of course, there were places we went to listen to music. A lot of outdoor concerts...mini-concerts, I guess. Musicians used to get together in the town parks and some of the little pubs and kind of...jam, I guess."

Luke nodded dubiously, then studied his mother carefully.

"I'm sorry you didn't get to see your friend this time, Mom," he said at last.

"You mean Skip?" Emma asked.

"Yeah, him, "Luke said.

"Oh well," Emma remarked casually, as she pulled onto the ramp leading to Route 6, "I should have tried to let him know I was coming ...You know, made a specific plan to connect."

"Of course, I wasn't even sure he'd be out here," she continued, "and for that matter, I wasn't even exactly sure how to get in touch with him."

Luke seemed surprised.

"Well, how do you usually get in touch with him?" he asked.

"Actually, I don't," Emma confessed, "at least I haven't recently. We used to write back and forth all the time, but then, you know, things happen, people drift apart."

"But I thought you said he's the one that told you Standish Village was for sale," Luke persisted.

"Right, he did," Emma said, "but that was something he wrote in a Christmas card, and I ...well...I didn't write back."

"Why not?" Luke asked.

"Because," Emma replied patiently, "I didn't know where to write. He didn't put a return address on his card, and well...he travels a lot for work, so I wasn't sure where he was...is...right now."

Luke briefly contemplated this information, then turned to look at his mother again.

"What does he do?" he said.

"Do?" Emma asked.

"Yes," Luke declared. "What's his job? That he travels for? What does this guy Skip do for a living?"

"He's a marine biologist," Emma stated firmly. "And he goes all over the world, you know, researching things."

"What things?" Luke asked.

"I don't know!" Emma said. "Marine things, I guess."

Luke shook his head wearily and for several miles, they rode in silence.

"You know, Mom," Luke commented at last, "for some guy who's supposed to be...how did you put it? Your best friend in the whole world? You sure don't know much about him."

"Kinda seems that way, doesn't it?" Emma replied sadly.

Just then the radio ceased its static hum and a Matchbox 20 song burst forth in perfect clarity.

"All right!" Luke said, "finally some real music!"

And with that, he reached forward and turned the volume up full. Then he leaned back, closed his eyes, and began to hum along with the song.

By the time they reached the Mass Pike, Emma had already run through their earlier conversation in her mind more times than she could count. Luke was right, of course. Why didn't she try to contact Skip and let him know she was coming to the Cape? In fact, why, exactly, hadn't she tried to find him all these years, especially after seeing him that time in Florida, and knowing somehow that things were okay between them, despite what happened that long ago summer night back when they were in college? Even though she didn't share this with Luke, it had been much longer than she wanted to admit since she had been the one to actually write to Skip...or even try to...than it had been since he wrote to her.

In fact, even though she had hinted to Luke that the Christmas card was part of an ongoing communication between her and Skip, it was more like a one-way contact, where he would touch base with her every so often, but where, embarrassingly now it seemed, she had not made the same effort in return. Again, Emma tried to tell herself it wasn't her fault, that she didn't have an address to write to, even if she wanted to, but something told her this was just a cop-out on her part.

Of course, maybe "wanted to" was the key. That last time she and Skip had actually been together for any meaningful length of time, before the Florida encounter, that is, was the summer she and her friends spent on the Cape. It was memorable, but definitely in the wrong way. It was nearly a week after the evening she and Skip spent out on his boat and Emma's subsequent encounter with David that they eventually saw each other again.

It wasn't exactly like Emma was trying to avoid Skip...at least that's what she told herself at the time...she was just...busy. First there were the extra shifts at the pub after one of the other servers quit, and then there was, well, David. He was her boyfriend after all, and she had promised him that evening outside the carriage house that she'd spend some time with him, when she wasn't working that was. Then, of course, after a few days, she really couldn't put off seeing him any longer.

As it turned out, both Jen and Amy knew where the house was that David's friend's parents owned. In fact, unbeknownst to Emma, they had already been there the night that Emma was out on the boat with Skip.

"Sorry we didn't say something sooner," Amy protested, when Emma found out where they had spent that evening. "We just weren't sure how things were between you and David."

"Also," Jen scoffed, "let's keep in mind that you're not the only one who knows any of these guys. Did you forget that we all go to the same college?"

What Emma did remember, actually, was that Jen had briefly dated the friend whose parents' house it was, and that Jen was the one who broke off that relationship. But she decided it would be better not to bring this up.

"Okay," Emma told her friends, "you're forgiven. But after David showed up here all missing me and being sorry and everything, I think I owe him another chance. And maybe if I just go over there and, you know, apologize, we can get things back on track."

Amy and Jen exchanged a suspiciously guilty glance.

"What?" Emma demanded. "You don't think I can be forgiving? Or do you think I'm having some "thing" with Skip? I told you, we're just old friends."

Amy hurried across the room and clutched both of Emma's hands in hers.

"Oh no, god no, Emma," she said. "It's nothing like that. We were just...we thought..."

"We think," Jen said, turning and opening the refrigerator behind her, "that you are too good for him"

"For either of them!" she declared, as she pulled out a bottle of Chardonnay. "Now let's drink to girl power!"

Emma smiled.

"Okay," she said, "let's do that!"

"Right on!" Amy agreed, although, as Emma recalled later, there was a certain degree of hesitancy in her response.

It was while they were sharing the bottle of wine on the patio behind the carriage house that Amy accidentally revealed the location of the house David and his friends were sharing.

"It's actually right down the road," Amy had explained and then laughed.

"Thank God for that," she added, "since we definitely needed to walk home the other night."

"Good to know," Emma told her.

"Why?" Jen asked, "are you thinking of paying your sort of, kind of, maybe still boyfriend a visit?"

Emma shrugged.

"I was pretty mean to him the other night," she said. "It seems like he was really sorry about blowing me off back at school...God, he actually told me he *missed* me, and what was it he said? He couldn't believe how *lost* he was without me?"

She shook her head.

"Maybe it's just the wine talking," she went on, "but it sure sounds like he was trying to fix things between us. I mean, we've been together a long time...maybe he's decided that he's been taking me for granted and wants to do better."

She looked up at her friends hopefully.

"Well, you never know," Jen remarked as she took another swig of wine. "People change."

"And you are definitely worth it, girl!" Amy added enthusiastically, a little too much so, Emma remembered thinking at the time. If only she hadn't been so impulsive, Emma thought...slept on it or something, before rushing over to hug and forgive David for his reckless actions.

After all, wasn't it David's spontaneous behavior that attracted Emma to him in the first place? How he would appear abruptly at her dorm room door with a picnic and a bottle of wine, and whisk her off to some romantic spot for the afternoon? Or how he would suddenly decide they should rent motor scooters and explore the nearby countryside, stopping at a remote little café for a quiet off-campus lunch?

It was in this frame of mind that Emma set off for the house where David was staying, just as it was beginning to get dark. It wasn't hard to find...Amy was right, only a short walk away. But by the time Emma reached the address Amy had written down for her, and started up the stone walk, the sun had completely slid below the horizon and the randomly scattered streetlights were starting to glow softly all around her.

The place was indeed large, just as David described, but it was hidden from the street by a huge leafy hedge, and set back far enough to suggest a natural feeling of privacy. A long front porch anchored by two hanging porch swings at either end lined the front of the house, with an array of rockers, side tables, and Adirondack chairs filling the space in between. While the massive wooden front door was flanked by two picture windows, it was clear that the main focus of the property no doubt stretched off the rear, where a sizeable deck overlooking the water was just visible through the glass.

Emma walked up the solid granite steps to the front door, and seeing no doorbell, raised her hand to knock.

"Emma?" someone called from the far end of the porch. Startled, she turned in the direction of the voice and squinted into the semi-darkness. There, together in one of the porch swings sat two figures; very close together, in fact, and when the one on the left abruptly stood, he clearly did so while untangling his arm from around the shoulders of the other. Then he strode quickly in her direction, until the light by the front door illuminated his features enough for Emma to recognize who it was.

"David?" Emma said. "What are you...I mean where...Who is..."

Slowly she took in the ramifications of the scene before her, as David shifted uncomfortably from one foot to the other.

"It's not what you think," David began, but Emma had already turned away, and begun hurrying back down the porch steps behind him.

"Emma, wait!" David called after her, but Emma kept going...down the walk, through the opening in the shrubbery, and out onto the sidewalk, tears streaming uncontrollably down her checks.

"It's not like it looks!" David shouted, as he reached the sidewalk. "She was just...she needed to...her boyfriend..."

"Stop!" Emma yelled without turning around, "just stop!"

Then she raised both hands in the air, and started to walk faster until she had turned the corner and escaped into the darkened streets beyond. By the time Emma reached the carriage house, she had stopped crying and was simply shaking with anger. Just who did he think he was! She demanded of herself. Being all sweet and loving and wanting her to come and spend the night, then suddenly with another girl?

As she stomped furiously down the shell driveway, Emma was somewhat relieved that there was no sign of Amy's car. Hopefully wherever she was, Jen was with her. Emma just wasn't in the mood to deal with her roommates' sympathetic murmurings, or worse yet, their "I told you so" attitudes.

No light came from the main house, not did there seem to be any coming from the apartment, something that might have annoyed Emma at another time, but for now, she was content to slip inside unnoticed. Nevertheless, as she approached the carriage house, the moon cast its quiet glow on a figure sitting on the bench outside the door. Oh no, she thought, could David somehow have gotten here first? She hadn't noticed his car out front. But then maybe someone gave him a ride. Damn! Now what?

But as Emma drew closer, the person on the bench turned slightly in her direction, and instead of her stocky, dark-haired boyfriend, this guy was obviously taller, and even in the dim moonlight, clearly had a full head of curly red hair.

"Emma?" he said. "Is that you?"

"Skip?" Emma asked. "What are you doing out here?"

Skip stood hesitantly.

"Waiting for you?" he suggested, at which point Emma again started to sob uncontrollably.

"Emma!" Skip cried, as he reached forward and taking both her hands in his, pulled her down on the bench beside him. "What's wrong? What happened?"

Then he leaned back and studied her carefully.

"It was him, wasn't it?" he declared. "Your so-called asshole boyfriend! What did he do now?"

"Nothing!" Emma sobbed. "He didn't do...it was all my fault!"

"Your fault?" Skip said. "What are you talking about? How could you be this upset for something that was your fault? I don't get it. The guy's a jerk, Emma. When are you gonna figure that out?"

Emma pulled away angrily.

"Don't even say that, Skip," she said. "You're the one that doesn't get it. You don't even know David, for Christ's sake, and here you making some stupid comment...calling him names, even!"

Skip released Emma's hands and looked out into the night.

"As a matter of fact, I do know him," he replied calmly, turning his head slightly, so that the moonlight fell on the side of his face. Under his slightly swollen right eye, and along his cheek an angry purple bruise was just beginning to yellow.

Emma gasped.

"What happened to you?" she demanded, gently touching his face.

"Your boyfriend happened to me," Skip said.

'You picked a fight with him?" Emma said, "Why would you do that? Especially since you obviously lost."

"First of all," Skip remarked, "I didn't pick a fight with him...more like he started the fight. And secondly, I wasn't even doing anything to cause it."

"In fact," he went on, "I was feeling kind of bad about the way I acted that night after we were out in the boat...like I was sort of rude to him, you know?"

"Ya think?" Emma scoffed.

"So anyhow," Skip continued, ignoring her response, "yesterday, he and some of his friends came down to the harbor...and they were looking for a ride out to one of the moorings...so, you know, I figured, what the heck? I owe it to Emma to try and fix this."

"Okay," Emma said, a bit more calmly. "Then what?"

Skip shuffled his feet nervously.

"So, I was all cheerful and asked them could I give them a ride to their boat," he said. "And then David, he looks at me sort of like he thought he recognized me, and says 'hey, aren't you that friend of Emma's'?"

"And so I said, yeah, that's me!" Skip paused and looked at Emma expectantly.

"That doesn't sound so bad," Emma replied cautiously, "so I don't get..."

"Wait," Skip told her, "there's more. David, he kind of glares at me and then says, 'you better stay away from her, got it?'"

Then he paused.

"Did I happen to mention that some of the 'friends' with him were girls?" Skip said, making air quotations with his hands at the word "girls."

"So?" Emma said, "So what? So some of them were girls. What's your point?"

"Well," Skip said, "when one of those so-called 'friends' started snuggling up to him, I couldn't help myself...I just yelled something at him."

"What exactly did you say?" Emma demanded.

Skip hesitated, then picked up Emma's hand before he spoke again.

"I told him that if he ever hurt you he'd be sorry," he muttered.

Emma jerked her hand away.

"Why did you do that?" she cried. "And what the hell business is it of yours in the first place?"

"What do you mean what business is it of mine?" Skip demanded. "It's always been my business what happens to you...ever since...ever since...Standish Village."

"And by the way," he added, "that's not all the jer...David...said."

Emma stared at him silently.

"Go on," she said.

"He said he could have any girl he wants and that you were just lucky that he happened to pick you," Skip declared. "At the same time he had his arm around his so-called friend, I might add."

"That's when I hit him," Skip mumbled staring down at his feet.

Emma stood abruptly.

"So what?" she said, turning and facing Skip fiercely. "So maybe it's true...so maybe he could have other girls and he did pick me. That's a good thing, you idiot. That he wants to be with me, no matter who else is around!

"And by the way," she added, "there's nothing wrong with him having friends who are girls! Look at us! We're just friends."

Skip said nothing. Then he stood as well.

"Are we, Emma?" he asked. "Are we just friends? Because even if we are, you got a funny way of showing it. But now that I think about it, maybe you always have."

Then he turned and started down the driveway, the shells crunching defiantly under his feet.

"Oh, and by the way, Emma," Skip called over his shoulder, "just for the record, I actually won."

Then he disappeared into the side door of the main house and was gone.

Fuming, Emma dug her apartment key out of her pocket and shoved it furiously into the lock, but in doing so, happened to glance down at the bench on which she and Skip were sitting. In his haste to storm away angrily, it appeared that Skip had left some sort of package behind.

Emma leaned over and picked it up, then switched on the light inside the door to examine the contents. No doubt some package he was delivering to one of her roommates, she thought as she pulled open the paper wrapping. Inside was an artfully arranged bouquet of bright blue hydrangeas, surrounded by green leafy stems and tied together with a white ribbon. Tucked into the mass of color was a small envelope.

Emma set the bouquet on the stairs leading to the apartment, turned the envelope over, and gently sliding her fingernail under the flap, removed the card inside. Even now, as she and Luke drove down the Mass Pike towards home, she could still remember exactly what was written there.

"Emma" the card read, "Don't forget the 'winding roads that seem to beckon you, miles of green beneath a sky of blue.' That's what makes 'that old Cape Cod' special...among other things ...one of which will always be you. Skip"

Emma stared at the message briefly, then stuffed it and the bouquet back in the paper wrapping and yanked open the outside door. In the faint light of the fading moon, she strode purposefully around the back of the carriage house to the large metal trash can located there, jerked off the heavy tin cover, and crammed the remains of the bouquet inside. Then she turned away, marched furiously back to the apartment, and went inside, slamming the door behind her.

"I am done with men!" she shouted up the empty stairway.

Later, when Amy and Jen returned to the apartment, Emma rolled over on her cot and pretended to be asleep. Wisely, neither of them chose to wake her.

Of course, she and David eventually made up, and he had explained everything...how the girl with him on the porch was, indeed, just a close friend and how her boyfriend had just dumped her, which was why he was consoling her that night; and even how she told him that "Emma was so lucky" to have such a kind and understanding boyfriend. David had also explained how there were five of them at the dock when Skip offered to ferry them to their mooring, and how Skip was actually "seriously hitting" on one of the girls, which is what really caused the fight (which "wasn't even with me, by the way," he added).

"You need to pick your friends a little more carefully," Emma remembered David telling her a couple nights later when they were snuggled in the hammock behind his friend's house. Sadly, Emma thought now, the guy had no idea how right he was, only just not in regard to Skip.

She tried to make up with Skip anyhow; after all, they had been friends for years. But when she finally went over to the main house to apologize, Skip's mother just looked slightly confused.

"Skip went back to school, Emma," she said, smiling sadly. "I just assumed he told you he was leaving."

"Apparently there's a summer session course he decided to take," she added uncertainly, then stood silently in the doorway.

"Oh yes, of course," Emma remembered replying quickly, "we just talked about it the other day. I must have gotten the dates mixed up."

Then she forced a cheerful smile.

"I'll just give him a call later and see how things are going," she said, before rushing off to work.

Now, as she drew closer to home and farther from the Cape, Emma wondered if there were just too many memories back there; if maybe the idea that she could buy Standish Village and live happily ever after on the shores of White Pond were simply some sort of childhood fantasy that neglected to take her more painful recollections into account.

She glanced over at her son who appeared to have fallen asleep, his head leaning crookedly against the passenger side window. Well, she thought, I guess it wasn't all bad...after all, look what eventually came out of the whole David thing. Then Luke opened his eyes, looked at Emma, and smiled.

"Eyes on the road," he said, still grinning. "Eyes on the road, Mom."

"Right," Emma said, looking straight ahead once again, and then she smiled as well.

Erni Johnson

Chapter Fifteen: The Decision (2003)

"So, how did it go?" Emma's brother, Stephen asked when he called on Tuesday morning. "Are you house poor yet? Or is it Village poor?"

"Oh hey, big brother," Emma said, propping the phone between her ear and her shoulder. Geez, she thought, as she began pulling things out of the laundry basket and dropping them in the washer, how can two people acquire so much sand in their clothes in just four days; this was, of course, in addition to what she'd already dumped out of their duffle bags.

"Well," she told Stephen, as at least half of Chatham Light Beach slipped from the pocket of a pair of Luke's jeans and cascaded to the laundry room floor. "I guess you'd say the jury is still out on that one, though there seems to be quite of bit of lobbying in both directions."

"How so?" Stephen asked. "Wait. Let me guess. The teenage boy is radically opposed to anything that will take him away from his friends with whom he basically has no conversation beyond 'didja see last night's game?' and 'what kind of pizza do ya wanna order?'"

Emma laughed.

"That's a pretty accurate description," she said, "you must have had some experience with being a teenage boy."

"Not a real one," Stephen replied, "but I was Joel's brother."

"Actually," Emma explained, "and surprisingly, I must admit, Luke seems somewhat ambivalent. Truthfully, I think he liked it out there more than he expected to."

"He took a lot of pictures," she added, "and he also reported that the whole place 'had some pretty good vibes,' whatever that means."

"Seriously?" Stephen said. "Who is that kid and what have you done with my nephew?"

"Oh, come on," Emma teased, "you gotta admit that even you were once "in love with that old Cape Cod.'"

"Emma," Stephen declared, "if you don't stop quoting that stupid song, I'm going to have to cut you from my Christmas list."

"Oh gee," Emma said, "you mean I won't get any more half broken lamps with weird fringe on the shades? Or teeny tea cups that don't match each other or anything else?"

"Yuck," Stephen went on, "all that sand stuck in your bathing suit and salt water drying out your skin? And eating disgusting things in shells for dinner? The place is my worst nightmare."

"Well anyway," Emma said, "Joel was the nay vote...at least I think he was...kinda hard to tell."

"Why?" Stephen asked. "What did he say?"

"Well, you know, Emma," Emma replied, lowering her voice to a stern male level, "Dad didn't leave us this money to fritter away on some pipe dream. Make sure you consider your options carefully."

Stephen burst into laughter.

"You sound just like him," he said. "I might even consider enduring sand in my crotch just to hear him sputtering about your foolish decision."

"Yeah, well, I guess he does have a point," Emma admitted. "But there are some viable opinions on the other side as well."

"Really, who?" Stephen inquired. "And don't say Jim, because I don't recall him being given a vote."

"Even though he's still my favorite?" Emma said. "Nope, actually the yea votes came from some people I met when I was out on the Cape."

"People you just met," Stephen declared. "And they are somehow important to your decision because...?

Emma hesitated.

"I don't know," she said, "maybe because being with them somehow made the whole idea just seem right."

"I'm not saying their opinion is what matters most," Emma added hastily, "It just gives me something more to think about, that's all."

"Well," Stephen remarked gently, "as my favorite brother would say, consider your options carefully."

"He's your only brother," Emma retorted and hung up.

What options? Emma asked herself later as she finished folding the now sand-free clothes from the weekend and then stood staring in the refrigerator for a dinner possibility.

She could finish packing all her mismatched glasses and plates, and the few pieces of furniture that were actually hers, and drag them to some other low-priced excuse for a home. And she could sign the teaching contract that was currently lying on the counter with the day's mostly junk mail (if not actually part of it), and make pretty much the same salary as she did last year...the one that barely covered the monthly bills. That way maybe she could stash some money away for Luke's college tuition, or even take him on the trip to the Caribbean that he seemed to be lusting after, or at the very least, buy the two of them a condo in the nicer part of town, and put away some actual savings.

Or, Emma concluded, I could do something I want to do for a change, instead of what everyone else wants me to do. After all, she was practically 40 years old and so far, her life had been one long progression of trying to fill someone's expectations without considering many of her own. As she pulled a selection of omelet ingredients out of the refrigerator, Emma glanced over at the answering machine on the other side of the room. Setting the pile of vegetables and the carton of eggs on the counter next to the sink, she crossed the room and pushed the play button. Since she had already listened to the messages once, the light indicating they were there was no longer blinking. But Emma had yet to erase them and now, after the conversations with both her brothers, she wondered if they might offer a new perspective.

Emma fast-forwarded past the first message...the one from her landlord reminding her that she needed to plan to move soon as the buyer was anxious to "remodel." Yeah, how come no one was "anxious to remodel" when she and Luke moved in, she wanted to ask. The second message, though, was a cheerful communication from Ted Parker, the Cape Cod real estate agent.

"Hello!" Ted Parker bellowed cheerfully after the beep. "Hope you had a great trip home! And sorry I couldn't meet you at the storage unit...you know how it is, busy, busy, busy!"

"But anyhow," he went on, after a brief awkward silence (what, did he think I was going to answer him? Emma wondered), "I was just interested to know if you had any more questions...you know, about the property, about Standish Village?"

"I'd be happy to answer any you have," Ted Parker added, exuberantly, "or...or...you know, talk more. And by the way...from what you told me, this just so seems like the perfect opportunity for you...and I don't want you to, you know, miss it, I guess."

Again, there was a brief silence.

"There's been quite a bit of interest in the place lately," he continued then, "lots of interest, actually, so you don't want to...lose this opportunity or anything...that is if..."

At this point it appeared that either Ted Parker had used up the allotted message time or run out of sales pitch...Emma couldn't figure out which. A lot of interest? She thought, as she pressed the pause button. Wait, hadn't Ted Parker mentioned that Standish Village had been on the market for years...what was it he said, somewhere between eight and ten years? Then where did all this alleged new "interest" come from, anyhow? Emma pressed the pause button again and the next message played.

"Hello?" the woman's voice said. "Wait, is this here one of them machines? I can't hardly tell anymore if someone's answering the phone or if it's just some recording. Dear god, what is this world coming to?"

"Anyway," she continued after an expectant pause, "this here is Alice...you know, the storage place lady? Hope you don't mind but Ted gived me your number, just in case...well, you know, you wanted to talk. About the furnishings, I mean...the stuff from Standish Village."

"Though seriously," she continued, "what's to talk about? Basically, you seen everything, well almost everything...but the rest is all like what ya did see."

At this point, Emma started to wonder how it was that Ted Parker seemed to have reached a time limit and yet Alice was able to ramble on without the machine cutting her off. Then she realized Alice was still speaking.

"I was talkin' to Charlie yesterday," she said. Emma could just picture the woman settling into a flowered armchair with a cup of tea...or more likely, in her case, a can of beer...as, after her initial trepidation regarding answering machines, she seemed to be warming to the whole technology.

"You remember Charlie, right?" she babbled on. "He says he met you out at the bandstand and that you was the one considering taking over Standish Village after poor Gordy...well...passed. And how you had some old time connection with the place?"

"Oh, I can't remember exactly what he said," she admitted. "Comes with gettin' old, dear. But the point is that he and I, we both think your plan to bring back the old place sounds near perfect and if we can help in any..."

At that point, mercifully, the message ended with a decisive beep.

"Finally," Emma responded aloud, a bit ungenerously, she realized after the fact. After all, the woman had given her that perfect pie. Before she could press pause again, though, another beep sounded and a fourth message came on. Huh...Emma thought, I didn't realize there was another message on here.

"Hey, hello there, it's me," the male voice announced, after which followed a garbled statement and then a rush of static, in the midst of which only a few words were actually intelligible.

"I...sure...this...right number... got from...long time no...so happy...Standish...very cool...that old Cape Cod..." Then there was another beep and the message ended.

Emma stood and stared at the answering machine. Could it have really been him? Calling her, after all this time? And how did Skip get her number? Or even hear that she went to the Cape?

Emma was still staring at the silent machine when Luke walked in the back door and kicked off his sneakers.

"Hey Mom," he announced cheerfully. "What's for dinner?"

Emma looked up and saw her son staring at the pile of ingredients next to the sink.

"Uh..." he said hesitantly, "Wanna order pizza?"

"That sounds good," Emma replied, as she crossed the room and gathered the remnants of the omelet plan and quickly returned them to the refrigerator.

"Sausage and mushroom?" she suggested.

"Perfect," he declared, then headed off down the hall to his room.

"Let me know when it gets here," he called over his shoulder.

Later, after she and her son had demolished the large sausage and mushroom pizza (right down to the crusts, no less), Emma leaned back in her chair and sipped contentedly on her glass of Merlot.

"So, what do you make of the phone messages we got?" she asked her son, casually.

"Phone messages?" Luke asked, as he crunched through the last of the remaining crusts. "You mean the one from Kirk the Jerk?"

This was Luke's favorite epithet for their landlord.

"Stop calling him that," Emma scolded, rather ineffectually she realized, then added, "not that one actually, the others...about the Cape thing."

"Cape thing?" Luke asked.

139

"Yeah, you know," Emma replied impatiently, "Standish Village? The place we went to look at on Cape Cod?"

Luke wiped his mouth on his napkin and finished his soda.

"Honestly, Mom," he said, "I just heard the message about how we have to move. I guess I didn't listen to the rest."

"What do you mean?" Emma asked. "They just all came on right after that one. You mean you pressed stop right after that one?"

Luke sat there silently, seemingly pondering his mother's response.

"Truthfully I didn't see any more messages," he said finally. "Are you sure you didn't erase the rest by mistake?"

Emma hesitated.

"Yeah, sorry," she said, "maybe I did."

"Well anyways," Luke said, as he pushed his chair back from the table, "is it okay if I go over to Zach's? He rented the new Terminator movie and I've been wanting to see that."

"Sure, that's fine," Emma told him. "just don't stay out too late."

"Sure thing, Mom," Luke said, and grabbing his jacket, he hurried out the door.

Later, after she had cleaned up the dishes and tossed the pizza box in the trash can outside, Emma went back to the kitchen and stared at the answering machine. Pushing the play button, she waited to hear the recorded messages.

"Hey Emma," came the voice of Kirk the Jerk, "how are your plans coming for your move? I've got some anxious buyers here, ready to remodel and so forth. Give me a call, okay?"

A plaintive beep followed and then silence.

Chapter Sixteen: Other Decisions (1987)

Emma found out she was pregnant less than a month after her mother died. It was late August and she was at home with her grieving father, and her two older brothers, who she was pretty convinced had decided they had put their lives on hold long enough. David was backpacking through Europe with two of his friends on what he called his "extended graduation celebration before facing the adult world." Emma, on the other hand, was painfully aware that her current condition was the result of the original graduation celebration, during which she and David had been a bit careless regarding birth control.

"It's all a question of timing," Joel pontificated, as the four remaining family members sat around the kitchen table, eating yet another of the somewhat tasteless casseroles contributed by their well-intentioned neighbors.

That's for sure, Emma thought, as she stirred the vaguely chicken flavored lumps of food back into the mushroom sauce currently congealing on her plate. Joel, however, being blissfully unaware of Emma's potential context for his remarks, was referring to his most recent business venture...or at least his latest proposal for one.

Joel was then 29 years-old and in the midst of what turned out to be a five year engagement to a strikingly attractive blond named Melissa (Missy for short), with an impressively bland personality. Having given up on traditional forms of higher education a number of years prior, Joel had now decided that his new "learn by living" mantra was a more practical approach to life. Lately, this plan included the potential purchase of the golf club where he had once mowed the greens as a teenager.

"What with Vince deciding to retire and all," Joel was saying, "because of his health and everything, I mean, it'd be the perfect time to make an offer...you know, basically lowball him when he's anxious to sell quickly."

"Ah..." Stephen remarked, pushing aside his barely touched serving of casserole, "the old kick-a-man-when-he's-down approach."

Having abandoned his floundering career path at the Museum of Modern Art (and thus no longer having a reason to pay an exorbitant rent on a fourth floor Brooklyn walk-up), Stephen was now living in his former bedroom in the family home. He had ostensibly come home to help care for his mother. Several months later, however, the "temporary" nature of his stay was significantly belied by the fact that his former bedroom was piled high with storage boxes containing the contents of his ex-apartment, and was inhabited, as well, by a large, hairy cat of indeterminate lineage.

Joel ignored his younger brother's comment, and turning expectantly toward his father, continued his explanation.

"The thing is," he went on, "I'm hesitant to plunge into this whole venture without, you know, a partner...someone to bounce ideas off and so forth."

Emma's father shook his head.

"Oh son," he said, "I'm much too old for that sort of thing. Why I'm planning on retiring soon, and the business world...well...it's changed."

"No room for an old fossil like me anymore," he added.

Joel looked down at his plate as if it was the first time he had seriously considered its contents, and then pushed it to one side as well.

"I'm not looking for money, Dad," he said softly. "Just, you know, moral support."

"Oh, well then," Stephen announced cheerfully, "if it's not monetary support you need, then I'm your man."

"Seriously?" Joel declared, turning to his brother in surprise. "Wow, I never thought…"

Stephen shook his head vehemently.

"No, of course not!" he retorted. "I'm just kidding, Joel. How could I possibly be of any use running a golf course? I mean, seriously, grown men chasing a little ball all over a bunch of wasted acreage, just to try and whack it into a tiny hole every half mile or so? Geez…how intellectual can you get?"

Joel sighed and leaned back in his chair.

"What about your friends?" Emma's father asked. "Surely some of your old buddies are still around, maybe looking for just this kind of business opportunity?"

"Also," Stephen pointed out, "you do have another sibling who just happens to now be a college graduate."

Emma had long since lost interest in the conversation and was absent-mindedly swirling the dregs of her wine around the bottom of her glass. Last she checked, she was pretty sure she liked Chardonnay, but just the smell of it right then was beginning to turn her stomach. At that moment, it abruptly occurred to her that the others had stopped talking and when she looked up from her wine, her father and brothers were all staring at her expectantly. But before she could open her mouth to ask why, she felt her entire serving of casserole, plus the wine that had topped it off, rise from her stomach into her throat.

"Excuse me," she said, and jumping up from the table, ran down the hall and into the bathroom where she vomited violently into the (fortunately) open toilet. The last thing she remembered thinking before sliding down on the cool tile of the bathroom floor, was that for once she was glad she lived in a house full of men.

The next time she opened her eyes, she was lying in her childhood bed, a washcloth on her forehead. As her vision cleared, she turned to her right and saw her father sitting in a chair next to the bed. He smiled, and handed her a glass of what appeared to be ginger ale, complete with "bendy straw". Then he opened a sleeve of saltines and laid it next to her on the bed.

"How far along are you?" he asked casually, as he pulled several crackers from the top of the wrapping and passed them to her.

"Too far," Emma grumbled as she sipped the ginger ale and reached for the saltines.

"How did you know?" she asked.

Her father shrugged.

"This was always the first sign for your mother," he said. "Suddenly, in the middle of dinner, she'd give me that surprised look, and then...you know...dash out of the room."

He punctuated the final comment by placing his palms together and sliding one hand in the direction of the bedroom door.

"Especially when you were...er...a bit of a surprise," he added and chuckled.

"But the best kind..." he said, as he leaned back contentedly. "Imagine, if we'd been more careful, I never would have had my little girl."

And then he smiled again and patted Emma's arm.

"I'm guessing you know this is a surprise," she said.

"Yup," her father said, "but as I found out with you, that's not necessarily a bad thing."

"Do the boys know?" Emma asked.

"God no!" her father scoffed. "Two of the most oblivious creatures on the face of the earth?"

"Your secret's safe with me," he added, squeezing her hand, "as long as you want it to be."

"Thanks," Emma said. Then she closed her eyes and went back to sleep.

By the time David was back from his European adventure, it was too late to do much of anything about it other than just tell him, a revelation that elicited a less than enthusiastic marriage proposal...what was his incredibly romantic response, "I guess I can marry you, if that's what you want?" Something like that.

And of course, Emma thought later, me and my infamous stubborn streak; if I'd just kept my mouth shut, I might have at least rustled up a little child support. But the fact that David seemed delighted when Emma lied and said she was getting an abortion, then said he'd give her a call in a couple weeks to "see how it went," was actually proof enough that the guy didn't belong in this child's life, regardless.

No, Emma thought a few days later, what she didn't need was a reluctant father forced into the role; but what she did need was a friend.

She hadn't spoken to either Jen or Amy since her mother's funeral, and her high school friends, while they, too, showed up to the funeral and expressed their sympathies, had long since drifted away as well. Besides, somehow it seemed pretty shameful to be looking for someone to confide in over an unplanned pregnancy when her family was still mourning the loss of her mother.

Plus, how would she explain the apparent disinterest of the baby's father, a guy who had been her steady boyfriend for nearly three years? She couldn't help but recall the looks exchanged by Jen and Amy on the Cape that summer, when she told them (enthusiastically, no less) that she and David had "worked things out" and were back together.

Nope, what Emma needed right now was a really good friend...a BFF who accepted and loved her unconditionally ...someone she could say anything to and would be there for her, no matter what happened or what she'd done wrong. Then, as she lay sprawled on the lounger on the patio one late August afternoon, it came to her...duh...her best friend in all the world, forever and ever, as he had once told her back when they were 11 years-old.

"I know you will think this is stupid," Skip wrote her after their second summer together at Standish Village, "but I just feel like we'll be best friends forever and ever. You know what I mean?" And yeah, at first Emma thought it sounded a little dumb, but before long she wrote back and simply said, "I know exactly what you mean!"

The problem was, the way she and Skip had left things. Try as she might to rationalize the whole episode in her head, chalk it up to stupid college stuff or whatever, the truth was that the last time they saw each other, or even talked for that matter, was two summers ago when they had that argument outside the carriage house on the Cape;

when she insisted on defending David, and then took the flowers Skip brought her and stuffed them in a garbage can, for god's sake. Obviously, he would have seen them in there when he emptied the trash the next day. What was she thinking?

And worse yet, after she told his mother she was planning to call him (because of course, she really was, right?) and then never did...because...because why? Because she and David made up, got back together, whatever, and well...you know...it just didn't seem like that whole thing could somehow fit with whatever it was she had with Skip.

Emma sat up abruptly on the lounger and buried her face in her hands. Is there anyone stupider than me? She thought. How could I not have at least called him? Apologized and said something like I was just so upset I didn't know what I was doing? Tell Skip he was still her best friend? And now, here she was, in desperate need of a best friend and somehow, she had simply, carelessly, let one go.

Then, something her mother always used to say came back to her; usually it was when she'd just had some big fight with one of her brothers, but actually it applied even more at the moment, now that she thought about it. "It's never too late to try and make things right," her mother would say, as she gently smoothed Emma's chaotic braids away from her face, "and if it doesn't work, well, at least you tried." And if Emma's father was there at the time, he would smile lovingly at the two of them and exclaim, "ah, the secret of my happy marriage!"

Emma stood, walked across the patio, and pulled open the sliding door to the kitchen. The house was empty. Joel had taken Emma's father to tour the golf club he intended to buy, and Stephen had gone along, because, as he put it, "there has to be at least one rational human being present." Emma eased across the room and tentatively lifted the receiver from the phone hanging on the wall next to the sink. Then staring briefly at the push button display, entered a cadence of familiar numbers.

It was a long shot, of course, dialing the phone number of the Peterson's carriage house where she and her friends lived that summer they spent on the Cape. But hadn't Skip joked about how the girls "took over" his apartment, while he had to live in his mother's "fussy, frilly guestroom" all summer? So, didn't it make sense that if Skip had just graduated from college at the same time she had, and was spending the summer with his parents, that this is where he would be staying?

Emma could hear the phone ringing on the other end of the line. This is ridiculous, she thought abruptly. Why would he be in the carriage house? He just graduated with some fancy degree in Marine Biology, no less, and was probably off sailing the high seas on some renowned research ship somewhere. What possible reason could he have for going back to…

"Hello?"

It took Emma a few seconds to realize that someone had answered the phone.

"Um…uh…hi," she mumbled, "is this…uh…is this Skip?"

"Yup, it's me," the male voice announced cheerfully, then paused.

"Emma?" he asked cautiously.

Fighting the urge to hang up and run back out into the yard, Emma slumped into one of the kitchen chairs and took a deep breath.

"Yes," she replied simply. There was silence on the other end of the line.

"Well," Skip said at last, "how are…?

148

"I just..." Emma interrupted, and then they both laughed awkwardly.

"Wow!" Skip said, "long time. How did you know I'd..."

"Oh, you know, "Emma said, "there's nothing like that old Cape Cod."

"If you spend an evening you'll want to stay," Skip agreed.

"But I'm just here for a couple weeks," he added, "so I'm glad you called when you did. I'm sorry about your Mom, by the way. My parents just told me about it last night, otherwise I would have..."

His voice trailed into silence once more.

"Thanks," Emma said. "It was kind of a relief, I guess. She was sick for so long, and I think in some ways, she was ready to go. It's still hard though, ya know?"

"Yeah, right," Skip said.

"So, what's ne...?" they both asked at once.

"Sorry," Skip said, "go ahead."

"No, you first," Emma insisted. "I'm guessing you graduated and everything...and are all set to take on the world?"

"Well, maybe some of it, at least," Skip told her. "I got a job anyhow."

"Really?" Emma said. "That's great! Doing what? I mean I assume something marine biology-ish, right?"

"I'm impressed," Skip exclaimed. "I can' t believe you remembered. Yup, I'm going down to Florida to a place called Harbor Branch...it's a research facility kind of like Woods Hole...and guess what?"

"I'm going to be working on an exploration vehicle," he went on, without waiting for Emma's response. "Kind of like that little sub, The

149

Alvin? You know, the one that went down to explore the Titanic? They've got another one just like it ready to go at Harbor Branch."

"Well, I'm not exactly working on it, but in the lab on the ship it launches from," he added, "analyzing what the thing finds...brings back...or you know, photographs and stuff. Pretty exciting huh?"

An image of a freckle-faced, red-haired little boy holding a large bullfrog in her face flashed briefly through Emma's mind. "Get that yucky thing away from me!" she remembered shouting at him at the time, but then seeing the crestfallen look on his face, she'd quickly softened and sitting next to him on the White Pond beach, had begged him to "tell me all about bullfrogs."

"That *is* exciting!" Emma told Skip now, with as much enthusiasm as she could muster.

"Oh, and I'm getting married!" Skip declared next, then he groaned. "Oh my god, Allison would kill me if she just heard the order in which I just listed all my exciting news."

"Married?" Emma repeated.

"Yeah," Skip said. "You'd love her, Emma. She's not at all like those dumb girls I used to go out with. Remember Caitlin?"

"Caitlin with a C?" Emma said. "How could I forget?"

"Allison is smart and funny, and loves being on the water," Skip continued, as if he hadn't heard her. "And she plays the piano and the guitar, and even speaks French...fluently, no less. Her father's a professor and they lived in Paris for a few years when she was a kid so..."

But Emma had stopped listening. Married? Skip was getting married? How could...when...why? It hardly seemed any time at all had gone by since his sister's wedding when she and Skip snuck away to the beach and drank champagne in the moonlight. Or for that matter, since they built castles on the sand at Standish Village, or rowed over to the little cove on the other side of White Pond to look for turtles.

"Maybe you could come!" Skip was saying now.

"What?" Emma asked.

"I said maybe you could come to the wedding," Skip repeated. "It'll be here on the Cape, but in December...a couple days after Christmas. Allison said she always wanted to get married by the ocean, but during the holidays so everything would be decorated for Christmas and the bridesmaids could wear red velvet dresses or something..."

"I forget the whole scenario," he confessed. "But anyhow, that's the first time I'll have off so..."

His voice dissolved into an awkward silence.

"Well, congratulations," Emma said at last, with what she felt was a lame attempt at enthusiasm.

"On all of it, I mean," she added. "It all sounds really perfect for you!"

"Thanks," Skip said quietly.

"But what about you?" he went on brightly. "I haven't given you a chance to tell me all about what's going on in your life? You graduated, I assume, then what's next? Some brilliant writing career? Or has your first novel already hit the shelves?"

"Of course," Emma remarked cheerfully. "Top of the bestseller list last week!"

"Truthfully, though," she went on, "I guess I'm at a bit of a crossroads right now. I got my degree and all that, but I'm not sure, I mean I can't decide exactly what to do..."

"I'm sure you'll figure it out!" Skip exclaimed. "You were always the one who knew exactly what to do, remember? Like the time we got caught taking the rowboat out at night at Standish Village, and you told your Mom that we were just star gazing and somehow the boat broke loose and floated off?"

Skip was laughing now.

"Or the time I dropped Stephen's radio in the pond and you told him one of those nasty geese grabbed it by the strap and pulled it in the water," he added. "That was too funny!"

"Yeah, that was funny," Emma said. "But the thing is now..."

"Hey listen, Emma, I gotta go," Skip interrupted. "But it was so great talking to you. How about I call you when Allison and I get down to Florida next week? Maybe you could even come and visit? After we get settled? I'd love for you to meet her."

"Um...yeah...sure...sounds great," Emma said.

"Nice talking to you too," she added, "but also, before you go, I just wanted to tell you I'm sorry about..."

But Skip had already hung up.

"...that night with David, and the flowers and not apologizing sooner," Emma told the buzzing dial tone. "And, by the way, you were right about him...like you always are...about everything..."

For the next half hour, Emma sat in the kitchen chair, holding the receiver, while a canned voice implored her "your connection has ended, please hang up the phone..." over and over. Finally, she stood, replaced the receiver on the hook, and wandered down the hall.

Later that afternoon, after Emma had retreated to her room, she heard a soft knocking on her bedroom door. Squeezing her eyes shut, Emma rolled over on her bed and faced the wall. Then she heard the door open gently and cautious footsteps, as someone crossed the room and sat down on the edge of her bed.

"Emma?" Stephen whispered, placing his hand carefully on her arm.

Emma lay silently with her eyes still tightly closed.

"I know you're not sleeping by the way," Stephen remarked. "So, I'm going to keep talking anyway."

"Of course, you are," Emma mumbled. "What else is new?"

Stephen chuckled softly.

"Dad told us," he said. "And I just want you to know I'm here for you."

Emma didn't answer.

"Also, Joel," he added. "Not like the moron would ever tell you himself."

Then Stephen sat there silently in the semi-darkened room as Emma, still refusing to turn over and look at him, began to drift into sleep. After a while, he stood and crept quietly toward the door.

"I know you are," Emma breathed as she heard the door open.

"And also, Joel," Stephen said, as he opened the door and stepped into the hall.

"Whatever," Emma whispered and smiled, when she heard Stephen chuckle once more.

Chapter Seventeen: Standish Village (2003)

It was hard to believe that only a month earlier, Emma had been flipping through the real estate ads, searching frantically for some semi-livable apartment rental for her and Luke, and now she was on the road heading for a place she actually owned. Not just a "place," but a whole village of places, and perhaps a whole new life.

It had all happened so fast...first the messages from Ted Parker, and of course, Alice...and Skip (at least she thought it was Skip...it must have been, right?) and then her talk with Luke. Suddenly everything just seemed to have fallen into place, and in a weird way, it was almost like it was meant to be; like Emma really didn't have any choice in the matter. Okay, she did have a choice, of course, but once Luke announced he was "totally on board" with the whole plan...well, then it seemed like this was what she was destined to do. And even though her brothers lacked the initial enthusiasm Emma hoped for, she had to admit that once the decision was made, they rallied around her supportively.

"You can just leave Luke with us on the weekends, you know, while you're out there working on the place," her sister-in-law, Missy exclaimed. "It will be no trouble at all and you know that the little girls simply love him!"

"It'll be good practice for when I have teenagers," she groaned in mock horror, "when he goes out with his friends and so forth, I mean."

"I'm sure I'll be up half the night worrying," she added.

Emma tried desperately to remember worrying about Luke when he was out with his friends on the weekends, and immediately became awash in a sea of parental guilt.

"I...um...Luke actually..." she stuttered, then gave up.

"He's a pretty good kid," she said finally. "And I'm sure he'll be on his best behavior."

Missy nodded and exchanged a knowing look with her husband.

"It'll be fine," Joel said, glancing sheepishly back and forth between the two women.

"You're letting Luke spend weekends with the Suburban couple of the year!" Stephen protested, when he heard the plan. "He'll be ruined for life!"

"Yeah, well, have you forgotten the time I left him overnight with you, and you went out to dinner with a friend, forgetting he was sleeping in your apartment?" Emma demanded.

"Emma, really, that was a long time ago, and he was just fine," Stephen protested. "Still sound asleep when I got home. And besides, I wasn't out that late."

"He was six," Emma declared.

"But a very mature six," Stephen pointed out.

"Besides," he added, "now I have Jim and let's not forget he's more responsible than all of us put together."

Emma sighed.

"How about every other weekend?" she said.

"What are we, getting divorced?" Stephen asked.

"Can one do that to her brother?" Emma replied and hung up.

In the end, it was Luke who solved the problem by offering to spend Friday night babysitting for his little cousins at Joel and Missy's, and then Saturday night at Stephen's (after going out with his friends), and then sharing Jim's famous Sunday brunch with them the next morning.

"Sorry about all this," Emma told her son, "but you know how the uncles can be."

"No problem, Mom," he said. "But you know, I am fifteen. You could just leave me by myself."

"Or," he added, when she gave him what he called the "mom look," "maybe I could just come to the Cape with you some weekends, and you know, help."

Certainly, she appreciated Luke's offer (as well as the confirmation it offered that he was indeed a "good kid"), but in some odd way, Emma felt like she had to go to Standish Village on her own, at least to begin with. It was her special place after all...well, hers and Skip's...and maybe at first, she might just want to unearth those memories alone. Maybe find out if being there again was some sort of answer to where her life was going, or where it had gone, even, and perhaps just find out if there was something out there to give her some direction. And something told her that initially, she had to do this by herself.

But also here was that phone message...the one she thought sounded like Skip...that she just couldn't get out of her mind. What if he was out there somewhere, on the Cape, and what if she could just see him and talk to him. Maybe after all these years they could be best friends again...because frankly, that was what Emma really needed right now.

"Hey Luke," Emma asked the night they came back from the Cape and she had listened to the phone messages, "what's that thing you do when you want to call back a phone number that just called you?"

"You mean star eight six?" he said. At the moment he was flipping through TV channels at the same time he was doing his math homework. Emma wondered if she should insist he just concentrate on his school work, but then realized that she was correcting a pile of vocab quizzes while watching him flip through the channels.

"Yeah, that's it," Emma said and slipped out of the room. But when she tried dialing it from her bedroom extension, it didn't exactly work out as planned.

"Parker Real Estate," the voice on the other end of the line announced, "Ted Parker here."

Which, as it turned out, was how Emma ended up on the Mass Pike that Friday afternoon in April, less than two weeks later. Ted Parker mailed the paperwork ahead of time so that Emma "could have a chance for her lawyer to look it over." But of course, Emma didn't have a lawyer...or the money for one, if the truth be known...to do the looking over, so when she called the real estate agent to tell him she'd be out the next weekend with "everything signed and in order," she had more or less read, organized (and signed) it completely on her own. Not like she'd ever tell Ted Parker that...in fact, she spent most of the drive to the Cape practicing her confident, mature attitude in the rear view mirror.

"Where will you be staying?" Ted Parker had asked her when they made the final plans to meet.

"Well...um...I thought maybe at Standish Village," Emma told him, "since, well, I'll own it and everything?"

"Oh yes, sure, of course," Ted Parker replied hastily. "How about I see if I can get a little furniture in one of the cottages...or something..."

He seemed definitely flustered. Maybe this is when I should become truly assertive, she told herself, especially if I'm about to became a businesswoman. Oh dear, she thought, I'm starting to sound like Joel.

"Yes," she replied firmly, nonetheless. "How about Cottage number 9? To furnish, I mean, for me to stay in this weekend."

"Absolutely!" Ted Parker declared. "I'll get right on it!"

And then he hung up.

It wasn't until Emma reached the Chatham exit off Route 6, that she realized she and Ted Parker had not discussed where they would meet to sign the final papers and complete the sale. Oh well, she thought, I'll just swing by his office and if he's not there, then I'll just go to over to Standish Village and settle in. He's bound to show up there sooner or later, she concluded; after all, I did tell him I wanted to stay in Cottage 9 tonight.

She did wonder if she'd been a bit rude, however, expecting him to clean and furnish her family's old cottage in just a few days' time. It might have been a wise plan to toss her sleeping bag in the back seat, just in case. Well, she could always go into town and stay at the inn if things went south, Emma supposed, but there was something about the idea of being back in that cottage, on the first night that it was really hers, that seemed somehow necessary.

Just then the little decaying plaza in which she had originally located Parker Realty, came into view ahead on her left, its worn sign still dangling uncertainly from the post by the road. Emma turned into the parking lot, bumping chaotically through a series of hidden potholes, and pulled up in front of the real estate office. A faint odor of sweet and sour pork drifted from the direction of "Hu Phon Yu's Authentic Canton Dining," as she stepped out of her car and onto the pavement in front of the three rundown establishments lining the sidewalk. From within the "Old Time Chatham Laundromat" the hum of dryers sporadically punctuated the air as well, even though the parking lot appeared to be empty of customers. Directly in front of her, Parker Realty was silent, dark, and deserted.

Emma stepped cautiously up on the curb, then, shielding her eyes with her cupped hands, she peered in the front window of Ted Parker's office. Just as it appeared from the outside, the place was indeed empty, but more than that, it didn't seem to be simply closed, but more like nonexistent. From what Emma could discern through the dirt-encrusted glass, there had been very little real estate business...or any sort of business, for that matter...conducted within these walls for some time.

"Ur ya lookin' for the real estate guy?" came a voice from behind her. Startled, Emma jumped back from the window and came face to face (frighteningly face to face, in fact) with an older gray-haired man standing next to her on the sidewalk. He carried a large plastic basket full of obviously dirty clothes, and seemed, quite cheerfully, to be on his way to somewhere else, though possibly not in the direction of completing his laundry chores.

"Oh...I ...ah..." Emma stammered, "yes, I guess I was. I mean, we didn't have an appointment or anything...at least here...in his office, but I...ah...just thought I'd stop by anyhow."

It occurred to Emma that she was babbling, but the gray-haired man didn't seem to especially notice.

"Well," he remarked cheerfully, "this office has been closed for some time. In fact, I think it's been years since anyone used it, and well, don't seem like no one took it over either, so..."

'Thanks," Emma said, as she quickly headed back towards her car. "I was just checking."

"Yup," the old man continued, as if she hadn't spoken. "So sad this whole little plaza shut down. But I guess that's just how things go nowadays...ever'thin' just gravitates toward the tourist stuff. This guy, Ted, though, so tragic how things all went for him. Such a fine fellow."

Emma had now reached her car and climbed inside.

"Well, thanks anyhow," she called, as she put the car in gear and backed out of the parking spot. But the old man did not appear to be listening. Instead he had turned, laundry basket in hand, and was staring at the row of buildings in the tiny plaza.

As Emma rolled down her window and drove back onto Route 28, it suddenly occurred to her that she no longer smelled Chinese food.

Chapter Eighteen: The Sandcastle

"So, were you able to get in touch with your friend?" Luke had asked, when Emma dropped off a pile of clean clothes in his room earlier that same morning, before she left for the Cape. Her son had gone as far as getting the duffle bag out of his closet, unzipping it, and tossing some clean socks and a tee shirt inside, before abandoning it in favor of stretching out on his bed and reading a book.

Emma's father once told her (on one of her more frustrating days as the mother of a toddler) that the best parenting advice he had to offer was never to wake a sleeping child or interrupt a teenager reading a book. At that moment however, Emma remembered thinking as she now drove through Chatham on her way to meet Ted Parker, she had been anxious to get on the road. This meant that Luke had to be dropped off at Joel and Missy's before this could happen.

"Why aren't you packed?" Emma demanded. "We have to leave in half an hour."

"Because," Luke replied calmly, as he swung his long legs around into a sitting position and placed the book on the bed next to him, "you are currently carrying all the clean clothes I have."

Emma looked down at the pile of tee shirts and jeans in her arms, then dropped them on Luke's bed.

"Well," she said, "now you have no excuse."

"Plus," she added, "you have some very nice khakis in your closet, along with at least five collar shirts that don't have pictures of rock bands on the front."

"And you want me to bring some of those," Luke conceded congenially. "Okay, I'll do the little preppie routine if it'll make you happy...at least when I'm at Uncle Joel's."

"It would make me happy," Emma said. Damn, she thought, why does he always have to be so agreeable; you can't even have a decent mom and teenager argument with this kid. Then she smiled.

"So, did you?" Luke asked, as he carefully separated a pair of jeans from the pile of clothes on the bed, then stood and walked over to his closet.

"Did I what?" Emma said.

"Get in touch with your friend," Luke remarked, pulling a pair of khakis from the closet and tossing them on his bed. "You know, the one in the picture I found, your friend from the Cape? The one whose parents' house we stopped at when we were out there, only they don't live there anymore and thus we were majorly trespassing?"

He looked up at his mother and grinned.

"Pretty sure that lady was about to call the cops," he added.

"You mean Skip?" Emma replied casually, ignoring Luke's last remark. "Actually, I tried to, if you really want to know. But it didn't work out."

"Work out?" Luke said absently, as he folded the khakis and stuffed them in his duffle.

"Yeah," Emma said. "I thought I had his phone number but when I tried it, it didn't turn out to be the right one."

What she didn't tell her son was that she had tried that *86 thing, hoping to reach Skip that way, since his message...or at least the one she thought was from him...was the last one on the machine. What she'd forgotten about, however, was the other call on the machine, the one that came in when she was unpacking the car. The caller didn't leave a message, just that proverbial anonymous click on the machine...the one that turned out to be Ted Parker, which she discovered after dialing the *86.

"When did you say I met him again...your friend from the Cape?" Luke asked as he zipped his bag.

"You don't have your toothbrush," Emma said. 'Go get your toothbrush."

"In Florida," she called after him as he headed down the hall to the bathroom, "the time you threw up on Space Mountain."

Delightful, she told herself. Now he will forever associate my memories of Skip, and for that matter, Cape Cod itself, with vomiting. But Luke had stopped listening and was currently rummaging through the medicine cabinet.

"Is okay if I take the toothpaste?" he yelled. "I hate that whitener stuff at Uncle Stephen's."

"Sure," Emma said, as she went into her room and surveyed her own packing efforts, "I'll pick up some more on the Cape."

It wasn't really fair to expect Luke to remember Skip and that afternoon on the beach in Florida, Emma realized now as she drove toward Standish Village. After all, it was her friendship, not his, and most of it had taken place long before he was born. Plus, Luke couldn't have been more than six years old when they took that trip with her dad and Stephen, if that.

They had gone there, actually, because Emma's father was considering buying a condo in Florida for the winter months, and invited them along for a "little vacation on the side," as he called it. Emma guessed that secretly her father didn't want to go down there alone, but she was happy to join him on the adventure, and on her budget, there certainly was no way she'd be able to take Luke to Disney World by herself. She had just gotten her first teaching job, in fact, and had made the independent step to move her and Luke out of her father's house and into her own, albeit tiny, apartment. Therefore, she also felt somewhat guiltily responsible for her father's abrupt decision to look at "retirement options" in Florida, where he'd be "part of a community."

Stephen's involvement in the whole event was a bit unclear to Emma, even now. At the time, he claimed he needed to make a "long-overdue visit" to an old college friend in Fort Pierce, but both Emma and her father knew he had serious misgivings that either of them could handle this trip on their own. Emma had to admit that he might have been right. Still, when her father announced he had "some real estate appointments" that afternoon that he clearly intended to keep on his own, Stephen reluctantly went off to lunch with his college friend, and Emma decided to take Luke to the beach.

"Are you sure you're okay doing this by yourself?" both Stephen and Emma's father asked anxiously, after carefully choosing and mapping out her route to the nearest beach.

"You can always come to lunch with Peter and me," Stephen offered.

"Oh right," Emma scoffed, "just what you thirty-something, button-down oxfords need for your lunch reunion, your scatterbrained little sister and her wiggly six year-old."

"We'll be fine," she added patting her dad on the arm and holding up the sheet on which Stephen had written the directions to the beach. "You've practically planned our whole day! All I need is to find a hot dog stand and stuff the kid with a little junk food, and all will be well with the world!"

Emma actually remembered feeling unusually free (not to mention adult), as she walked her son the few blocks to the beach, lugging their towels and sand pails, and happily swinging their hands between them. It had been as if she was truly a grown-up for the first time, just she and her little boy enjoying their beach vacation together. They found a spot near the water and dropped their towels where the waves could just barely reach their toes. Luke had been obsessed with the idea of building a sandcastle ever since they arrived in Florida, and Emma was determined to offer her expertise.

"First," she remembered telling him, "you have to dig the moat."

"The what?" Luke asked.

"The moat," Emma repeated. "It's like a little river that goes around the castle and protects all the people inside from invaders."

"Like space invaders?" Luke said.

Emma sighed. She'd forgotten that Luke had recently become obsessed with Star Wars when Joel brought over his VHS collection of movies.

"No silly boy! It's for protection from the Barbarians!" exclaimed a male voice above their heads.

Startled, Emma looked up, shielding her eyes from the bright sun now silhouetting the figure that had appeared next to them on the beach. Brushing the sand from her hands and knees, Emma stood and eyed the unfamiliar man warily. Maybe coming down here alone wasn't such a great idea after all.

Just then, the stranger stepped slightly to one side so that the sun was no longer at his back and his features came fully into view... along with his curly red hair. Then he grinned.

"Hey Emma," he said, "what the heck are you doing in Florida?"

"And who's this little guy?" he asked, his attention now drawn to the little boy digging furiously in the wet sand at his feet.

"Skip?" Emma said. "What...I mean, how...where did you come from?"

"Well," he said, "I actually live here and this is where I take my run every afternoon around this time, so I'm thinking maybe the question remains."

"Question?" Emma asked. "Oh, you mean what am I doing here?"

Skip stared down at Luke again.

"I'm...uh...building a sandcastle?" she went on, "with my son."

"Son," Skip repeated. "This is your son."

"Right," Emma said.

"Okay then," Skip replied, as he plopped himself down on the sand next to Luke.

"Then the first thing you have to understand," he told the little boy, "is that your mother has no idea how to build a sandcastle, and even if she pretends she does, it's only because I taught her everything she knows."

Later that afternoon, long after the construction of the fortress had been completed (and the "Barbarians" had indeed attacked with their giant stomping feet), Emma, Skip, and Luke gathered up the towels, and pails and shovels, and headed up the beach, away from the gently pounding waves.

"Do you need a ride?' Skip asked. "My car's right over here."

"No thanks," Emma said, "our hotel is only a few blocks from here, and the more tired Luke gets by walking there, the better evening I'll have."

"Is your...husband...back at the hotel?" Skip inquired casually. In the midst of castle building, he and Emma had managed to exchange news on their professional lives...hers as a new teacher and his as a marine research assistant...but neither had offered little by way of personal information.

"Um... no..." Emma said, as she continued walking.

"I mean," Skip explained, "I was just thinking that maybe we could all have dinner...you and him, and me and Allison? We know some great seafood places."

Emma hesitated.

"There actually isn't a him," she said at last. "Luke and I...we're on our own."

"Oh," Skip said, then he stopped and turned to face her.

"I'm sorry, Emma," he said, "I didn't know...I mean, I thought..."

"It's okay," she assured him, "I should have told you."

"Anyhow," she went on, "I'm here with my dad and Stephen, and...well...Dad went to look at some retirement places today, and I think maybe I should just hang out with them tonight...you know, in case Dad wants to talk about anything with us."

"I know," Skip replied and shrugged. "I mean, I know why you're here and I didn't just happen to be running down the exact beach you decided to go to."

"In fact," he added grinning, "I even got some very specific directions as to how to locate you."

"Like these?" Emma said, pulling the folded sheet of paper with Stephen's detailed directions from the pocket of her cutoffs.

Skip peered over her shoulder and chuckled.

"Nearly identical, in fact!" he declared, then shook his head.

"Actually," Skip confessed, as they started walking toward the nearby parking lot, "Stephen called me at Harbor Branch last week and told me when you'd all be coming down here."

"To be honest," he said, "I was surprised he even knew where I worked...I mean, I haven't seen or talked to him in years."

"Yeah, well," Emma admitted, "I might have mentioned it to him...you know, because Dad was looking at Florida retirement places and all that, and it...um ...reminded me what you said about moving here...the last time we talked, that is."

"He also said he thought you needed a friend right about now," Skip added hesitantly.

Emma paused.

"I might have mentioned that also," she said quietly. "It's just that I finally got my degree, and a job, and moved out of my Dad's house...which I'm really excited about... but I guess I'm finding out that it's a little lonely out there...in the real world, I mean."

"That's sort of what he told me," Skip replied. "But he didn't happen to mention the part about...um...you know..."

He looked down at Luke who was happily skipping along between them.

"Honestly?" Emma declared glumly. "He shouldn't have talked about any of it to anyone. It must make me sound pretty pathetic, right? Just what I need."

Skip said nothing and for a few moments they walked in silence.

"You don't seem pathetic at all," he said at last. "In fact, I know just how you feel. Just because things look great on the outside doesn't mean they really are."

"The whole single parent thing, for example," he went on "that can't be easy."

"It's a little tough on the playground," Emma said, then she turned towards Skip and smiled mischievously.

"I used to pretend I was his nanny," she said, "so I could chat with the other nannies...complain about our bosses and stuff."

Skip laughed.

"How'd that go for you?" he asked.

"Okay for a while," Emma said, "but just when I started making friends, Luke would call me Mommy and blow my whole cover."

Skip laughed again.

"Same old Emma," he said.

By that time, they had reached the parking lot and now stood facing each other awkwardly while Luke ran in circles around them making airplane noises."

"So listen," Skip said finally, as he pulled a crumpled receipt from his shorts pocket. "How about I give you my phone number and then you can call me...us...later...and maybe we can meet up tomorrow? Do you have a pen?"

Emma reached in her beach bag, dug around briefly, and finally produced a red crayon.

"Will this do?" she asked. Skip took the crayon and shaking his head, he scrawled a number on the back of the receipt.

"Same old Emma," he remarked affectionately.

"Yup," Emma replied grinning, "still the same old me."

"Okay so this is my car" Skip said, pointing to a battered red jeep parked near where they stood. "It was good to see you, Emma."

"Yeah," Emma agreed, "good to see you too."

"And we'll talk more tomorrow, okay?" Skip said, as he unlocked his car and opened the driver's side door.

"Best friends forever and all that," he added cheerfully.

"Right!" Emma exclaimed, taking Luke's hand and gently pulling him toward the sidewalk.

"I'll see ya when I see ya," she said.

"Not if I see you first," Skip replied. Then he got in the car, waved cheerfully, and drove away.

Of course, Emma neglected to tell Skip that she and her family were leaving for home first thing in the morning and thus she wouldn't be calling him to make dinner plans, or for anything else, for that matter. And when Emma got back to the hotel and Stephen asked her, a bit over enthusiastically it seemed, "so how was the beach?" all she did was smile and tell him, it was "nice," that may have been less than honest as well. Wisely, her brother chose not to pursue the subject.

I'll just call Skip when we get back home, Emma told herself at the time, and tell him we left earlier than we planned. Talking on the phone would be easier than face to face, she decided, especially minus the all too obvious presence of Luke and Allison.

Later, though, as she sat next to Luke on the plane, she suddenly remembered setting the crumpled receipt on her hotel bedside table and...and what? Did she pick it up again in the morning? Rummaging through her purse, all she could come up with was her wallet, keys, a nearly empty travel pack of Kleenex, a comb missing two teeth, and some very stale gum.

"Mommy," Luke said, tugging on his mother's sleeve. "I can't find my red crayon."

"Use a different color," Emma told him, as she returned the random array of items to her purse.

"But I need red," Luke insisted, looking down in despair at the unfinished drawing on the tray in front of him.

"Try purple," Emma sighed. "It's not red, but it's close enough."

"Sometimes if we lose something we think we need," she added, "we just have to find something that's close to what we need."

"Okay," Luke said, and picking up the purple crayon, he started to draw once more.

Chapter Nineteen: Cottage #9 (2003)

When Emma pulled into the parking spot next to Cottage #9, it was mid- afternoon and Standish Village sat quietly soaking up the unlikely sunshine of an early spring day on Cape Cod. There was no sign of Ted Parker's black Mercedes when Emma stepped out of her car and crunched her way across the crushed shell path that led to the steps of the cottage. Truthfully, she wasn't especially disappointed that the real estate agent had yet to arrive; in fact, she had looked forward to the chance she might have to be here alone...at least initially.

"Well hello there!" came a cheerful voice nearby, startling Emma into nearly stumbling over the bottom step.

"Hello?" Emma called, as she steadied herself against the railing and leaned to peer around the front of the cottage.

There, dressed in painter's overalls and holding a bucket of paint and a dripping brush, stood Charlie, the old man Emma met two weeks earlier at the Chatham bandstand when she and Luke took their initial trip to the Cape.

"Oh," Emma said, stepping back down onto the shells and moving closer to the smiling man. "Charlie, right?"

"You betcha!" Charlie exclaimed. "So nice 'a you to rememba'."

Emma stared down skeptically at the paint and paintbrush, and then back up at Charlie's expectant face. Once again, tufts of bushy white hair stuck out from under his cap, and bits of crusted white paint dotted his cheeks and clung to his abundant mustache.

"What a surprise to see you here!" she said finally.

Charlie looked confused.

"Didn't Ted tell ya?" he inquired.

"Tell me what?" Emma asked.

"That I'd be workin' here," Charlie announced and smiled. Then he waved the still dripping paintbrush in the general direction of the row of cottages behind him. "I'll be givin' all these here places a little facelift!"

"I started with this one," he went on, indicating #9, "cause I understands yer thinkin' a' settlin' in here ta begin with!"

"Least that's what Ted said," he added, somewhat subdued now.

Emma smiled reassuringly.

"That's so nice, Charlie," she said, "but I'm not sure I can pay...I mean, I haven't really figured out my budget quite yet, and..."

Charlie waved the paintbrush hand impatiently, sending tiny splashes of white on the layer of pine needles at his feet.

"No, no," he said, "you don't need to pay me nothin'! I just love havin' somethin' ta do. You know, keep me moving. Nice lady like you! I'm more an' happy to help out."

"I do gotta admit," he continued, leaning forward confidentially, "I also kinda got a soft spot for this ole place. Been deserted for so long, and back in the ole days...well, it was just such a happy little community. Couldn't stand seein' that slip away, ya know?"

Neither could I, Emma thought, so abruptly, in fact, that it startled her.

"Well, that's very kind of you," Emma said, quickly pulling herself together. Maybe the old guy really just needed something to do, some purpose in life, she thought.

"But maybe I can get you some help after you get started," she added. After all, she didn't want him to get overwhelmed. He was a such a nice old guy and there were fifteen cottages on the property, some fairly sizable.

But Charlie didn't seem to be listening. Instead, he stood wistfully gazing around at his surroundings.

"Yup," he mused, "people used to come back here year after year, bringin' their whole families sometimes. Not just their kids, but aunts, uncles, cousins...grandmas and grandpas, even."

"In fact," he went on, leaning in Emma's direction once more, "some folks say the guests even used to come back when they was no more...just 'cause they loved it so much, ya know? Couldn't bear to give it up, I s'pose."

Then he winked and grinned mischievously.

"What do you mean when they was...were...no more?" Emma asked, then her eyes widened. "Wait...are you saying the place is haunted?"

But Charlie had already turned and disappeared around the corner of the cottage.

Emma sighed and began climbing the steps of Cottage #9 once again. Crazy old man, she thought, and wondered briefly whether it was a good idea to let him keep working here. Oh well, what harm could he do really, right? Even if he did seem to believe in ghosts. Still, as Emma reached the porch at the top of the steps, she had the vague feeling that she'd heard something like this before about Standish Village.

The old cottage door squeaked and shuddered as she pushed it open. Even though it had been more than 25 years since she'd stood on that porch, it still looked much the same. Granted a sturdy pine picnic table replaced the rickety one that once stood in the far corner, and two bright white Adirondack chairs sat on either side of a glass topped table in front of the new picture window looking out from the cottage; nonetheless, a tiny tear in the porch screen assured Emma that things had not really changed all that much.

Someone had placed a bouquet of fresh flowers on the picnic table, and a small lantern in the shape of a lighthouse was perched on top of the glass one. If only Mom and Dad could see this, Emma thought sadly, as she ran her hand along the ledge next to the screen door. It was then she noticed that the tips of her fingers had brushed against a neat row of seashells lining the ledge. Why, this was exactly where she and her brothers always put their beach treasures! After, of course, their mother had forbidden them from bringing "those sandy, smelly things in this cottage!" Emma smiled at the memory. How nice that other children (and their mothers, she suspected) had continued the tradition.

Emma dropped her duffle bag on the floor of the porch, opened the cottage door and stepped into the front room. Not really knowing what to expect, she was pleasantly surprised by the scene confronting her. Once filled with a true cottage motif of stiff backed chairs, and wobbly tables topped with uncertain lamps, the room now boasted a deep cushioned couch, and wide soft chairs in sea blue hues. Sturdy white wooden side tables, supporting a variety of ocean themed lighting, embraced the other furnishings. Even the coffee table was strewn with decorative shells, and candles begging to be lit into a soft glow as soon as dusk descended. In the corner of the room, a new free-standing fireplace, its chimney snaking up to the ceiling and through the roof, was laid with logs and kindling waiting to be encouraged into an evening blaze.

It was then that Emma noticed a divider wall had been added between the living room area and what had been an alcove for the kitchen appliances. Although the two sections of the cottage's front room were now officially separated, the doorway between them was merely an arched opening, and a large space in the new wall created not only an easy view of the kitchen, but a bar between the two areas next to which several stools had been placed. From where she stood, Emma could also glimpse the addition of several shiny new appliances. These included a large stove, in front of which the ample backside of a woman bending over the oven was now visible. The smell of blueberry pie was also unmistakable.

"Alice?" Emma inquired tentatively.

The woman by the stove straightened and turned in Emma's direction...and sure enough, in her mitted hands she held a bubbling, steaming pie, fresh from the oven.

"Oh goodness, girl, you done startled me!" Alice exclaimed. "I weren't expectin' ya quite so soon!"

"Is that for me?" Emma asked eagerly, as she entered the kitchen.

Alice looked down at the pie in her hands.

"Why 'a course, my dear!" Alice exclaimed. "It's a welcome home present!"

"But ya need to let it cool a bit," she added, as she set the pastry on top of the stove.

Emma smiled.

"Of course," she said. Then she looked around the room.

"Everything looks so nice!" she told Alice. "I mean, when I told Ted I might want to stay here in this cottage, I never thought…"

Alice waved her hand dismissively.

"Oh posh," she said. "T'weren't that hard to just bring the furnishings in and fix things up a bit. We're all jist so delighted you decided to take over the place!"

Emma wondered who the "all" were to which Alice referred, but decided it might be impolite to ask.

"I saw Charlie outside," she said, instead. "Apparently he…umm…is planning on painting all the cottages and…uh…might that be…a bit much for him?"

Alice laughed and patted Emma's arm.

"Don't you worry about Charlie, hon," she said. "He may look like an old coot, but he works fast, and gits things done. 'Sides, I think he loves gettin' the chance to feel useful. All us older folks do, I 'magine. We've had our troubles over the years, and most folks 'round here don't think we're quite what we used to be."

Then she winked at Emma, took off the flowered apron she was wearing, and laid it on the counter by the stove.

"Now you jist get yerself settled in," she said. "Ted tole me he'd be along shortly."

"Alice," Emma began tentatively, "just now, when I was talking to Charlie, he said something about…about people coming back here…after they were…um…no more."

Alice cocked her head inquisitively.

"No more?" she said.

"Yeah," Emma replied, feeling a bit foolish now, "you know ...after they were...gone. Like ghosts or something."

Alice stared at Emma briefly, then threw her head back and laughed heartily.

"Rubbish!" she declared. "That ole man was just playin' with ya. There ain't no sech thing as ghosts."

Emma smiled awkwardly.

"I know," she said. "It's just that, well...it seems kind of weird that Standish Village was on the market for so long, you know, and I just thought maybe that was because...because people thought..."

"That the place was haunted?" Alice exclaimed and laughed again, as she moved over to the sink and turned on the faucet.

"Oh sure, some folks used to say stuff like they saw some strange things goin' on," she said, her back to Emma as she rinsed her hands under the running water, "but I think that were just for the publicity."

"Publicity?" Emma asked.

"Course," Alice replied, as she dried her hands on a nearby dish towel. "Young Gordy Anderson, the fella that inherited the place from his granddaddy? He figured he could sell his condos faster if folks thought the place was haunted...that'd they'd come and have a look see, because they was curious and all...and then the folks would like it so much here, they'd just buy themselves a cottage!"

"Oh," Emma said, shuffling her feet nervously. "So, you don't believe..."

"No, I do not!" Alice declared, as she moved toward the door. "And even if I did, I'd say be they be friendly ghosts."

"Friendly ghosts?" Emma asked. This was something she'd never heard of...if the place was indeed haunted, all she could picture was the horror movies she'd seen at the Cape drive-in; the ones Joel took her to once he got his license…and the ones she never told her parents about.

"Right…People who come back here 'cause they loved it so much," Alice explained, "so much they just couldn't stay away."

"Kinda like you!" she added, patting Emma's arm again.

"But I…" Emma began. Then, however, with what seemed to Emma far much too energy for a woman her age, Alice was across the room, and out the door.

"Thanks for the pie!" Emma called after her, but when she looked out on the porch, Alice had already disappeared.

Still somewhat shaken by her conversation with her new friends, Emma prowled through the rest of the cottage while she waited for Ted Parker to arrive. The two bedrooms in the back had also been upgraded with beach motif furnishings and bed linens, and crisp new curtains hung from the windows. Even the stark overhead lights had been replaced by the soft glow of lamps on bedside tables and bureaus. The larger of the two bedrooms, in which Emma's parents once slept, now boasted the addition of a tiny bathroom off the back, while the original bathroom in the hall that the five of them once shared had been newly renovated.

But the nicest surprise of all was when Emma opened the remaining door on the narrow hallway and peered inside. Expecting the little storage room that once sufficed as her childhood bedroom to have been restored to its original use, she was shocked to discover that it had, instead, been furnished as a small office. Along one wall and extending around the corner was a built in desk with an array of cupboard-like shelving above, a desk lamp arching across the center of its surface, and a professional looking office chair pushed underneath. Lined against the opposite wall was a row of wooden file cabinets, and next to these a small table on which sat a portable copy machine.

In the center of the back wall was the window Emma remembered and when she crossed the room and looked out, a tiny bird perched on a branch of the scrub pine still growing there seemed to be waiting for her to notice him. There was even a phone and answering machine on one corner of the desk next to the window, and when Emma picked up the receiver, a reassuring dial tone buzzed in her ear.

"I tried to think of everything you might need."

Startled, Emma dropped the receiver and turned in the direction of the voice. There in the doorway stood Ted Parker, his shiny dark suit replaced by khakis and a golf shirt, and his tasseled loafers by a bright white pair of Nikes.

"Sorry," Ted Parker said, "didn't mean to scare you. The door was open so I..."

'No, no," Emma said quickly, as she moved towards the hallway and smiled. "I was expecting you."

"It's just that...that everything looks so nice!" she exclaimed gesturing to the rest of the cottage. "I thought I was in for a weekend of renovations, but clearly you beat me to it!"

Ted Parker shrugged apologetically.

"Well, don't get too excited," he said, chuckling, "I got this cottage ready for you, but the others...well...they still might need a little work."

Emma smiled, and then as if on some hidden cue, they both turned in the direction of the kitchen from which the smell of fresh baked pie still lingered.

"Pie?" Emma inquired.

"I thought you'd never ask," Ted Parker replied.

Later, as they sat at the kitchen table, a half-empty pie dish between them, Emma signed the final papers for the purchase of Standish Village.

"Well," Ted Parker announced, as he piled up the paperwork and stuffed it back in his briefcase, "I guess she's all yours now. What's your plan?"

Emma wiped the excess blueberry from her mouth and dropped her crumpled napkin on the table.

"Plan?" she said.

"Yes," the real estate agent replied. "To get the place up and running, I mean."

"Summer season's just around the corner!" he added cheerfully, as he stood and snapped his briefcase shut.

For the first time, the enormity of actually owning *and* running a cottage colony struck her, and for a moment, Emma felt entirely overwhelmed. But there was no way she was going to admit this to Ted Parker, so she simply stood, shoved her hands in the pockets of her jeans, and smiled confidently.

"I've got some things already in the works," she declared cheerfully. "A couple months from now you won't even recognize the place!"

The images of the dripping paintbrush dangling from Charlie's hand and Alice in her overalls and blueberry stained apron popped briefly into Emma's head, but she just as quickly pushed them aside.

"I'm sure I won't," Ted Parker was saying as he ambled toward the porch door.

"Oh!" he said, turning back abruptly, "I almost forgot. A young fella come by today a'fore you got here. Says he used to come here as a boy. Knows your family, I think he said."

"What did he want?" Emma asked.

Ted Parker shrugged.

"Dunno," he said. "Lookin' for a job maybe? He looked like the handyman type, kinda. Jeans, boots, tool belt...you know the look..."

Emma frowned.

"Doesn't sound like anyone I know," she said. "Did he tell you his name?"

Ted Parker scratched his head.

"Maybe," he said, smiling apologetically, "but if he did, I don't remember it."

"He said he'd come back around later, though," Ted Parker added helpfully, then shrugged again and started down the steps toward his car. Then he turned back as if another thought had suddenly struck him

"Guy had a full head of curly hair," he remarked brightly. "Kind of reddish...I remember the hair 'cause it didn't really fit, ya know? Most 'a them handyman guys, they cut their hair real short...so it don't get in the way...when they're workin' I mean."

Emma nodded.

"Okay, well I'll watch for him," she said. Ted Parker turned again and waved carelessly over his shoulder as he continued down the steps.

How odd, Emma thought. She and her family hadn't been on the Cape in years, and now some guy drops by and says he knows my family? He must be thinking of someone else. She shook her head, and moving to the far side of the porch, she stood with her arms crossed and gazed down at the pond just visible beyond the thick growth of scrub pine.

Probably some friend of Joel's, she decided. That would be just like her eldest brother to act all doubtful and disinterested in her purchase of Standish Village and then recruit some buddy of his (or more likely pay the guy) to come out here and act like he was just looking for a job. Joel would assume that Emma would be desperate for the help and then afterward, when she paid the handyman what she could afford, Joel would just add to that amount on the side. Oh well, who could blame him, really. What did Emma know about fixing up this place anyhow? And when she thought about it, it really was kind of sweet of Joel to do this, even though it irritated her that Joel...both her brothers, in fact...still seemed to think she needed them to take care of her.

Then again, maybe she did. Emma liked to think she was a truly independent woman; after all, she did raise her son on her own, managing to become a teacher in the process, no less. She had a good, job, rented her own place, paid her own bills. But now, as she watched a flock of geese fly overhead and land on the little sand beach below, a flood of memories came back to her: Stephen teaching her to swim in that very pond, and helping her sound out hard words in her childhood books, right here on this porch; Joel showing her how to swing a croquet mallet, and wiping up the drips from the ice cream cone he bought for her, all the while assuring her that Mom wouldn't care how much she spilled on her clothes; and her dad, slipping into every image she could see, from when they first rowed over to the cove and watched the turtles, to sitting endlessly next to Luke at the kitchen table, as her son struggled with his math homework.

Clearly, she hadn't done this alone, no matter how many times she told herself that she had. And then, of course, there was Skip. It wasn't like Emma didn't have other friends; good friends like Jen and Amy, with whom she could talk about anything. Or even nowadays, her teaching colleagues always willing to help out when she became overwhelmed with the conflicting roles of full time educator and single parent.

And it wasn't like Skip was even around much after their early years as friends here at Standish Village. It was simply the fact of him. Of knowing that out there, even when communications were few and far between, there was someone who understood exactly who Emma was; someone who could finish her sentences before she even started them, and when the chips were down, no matter what she had done or said, would always be on her side.

It was now late afternoon, and the earlier sunshine was beginning to fade. Pulling a sweatshirt from her duffel, Emma decided a walk down to the pond might clear her head. The overwhelming sense of responsibility that had plagued her less than an hour before now seemed to have transformed into a surprising sense of contentment, and for the first time since she began this venture, Emma found herself more hopeful than wary of the future. Yet something continued to nag at her about the whole thing; something she couldn't quite put her finger on. Maybe seeing the calm, mirror-like waters of the pond and listening to the stillness of the impending dusk might be just what she needed to put her mind at ease.

But when she reached the little sand beach lining the shore of White Pond, Emma discovered she was not alone. Seated in one of the decaying wooden rowboats, his back to her, was a little boy, apparently oblivious to her presence. Dressed in a faded yellow tee shirt and rumpled jeans, his curly red hair reflecting the setting sun, the boy seemed somehow familiar, though Emma was not exactly sure why. There was just something about the way he looked out across the pond, humming softly to himself that reminded her of another moment in time.

Just as she was considering whether or not to speak to him, the little boy turned abruptly and smiled at her.

"Hi," he said cheerfully.

"Hi yourself," Emma replied as she moved closer. "Watcha doin'?"

The boy looked down into the boat and then back out towards the water.

"Nothing really," he said cautiously, "just kind of hanging out, I guess."

"I hope that's okay," he added earnestly, turning around to look at Emma again, "I mean usually...usually...there's nobody here, so I..."

"It's fine," Emma assured him. "I didn't mean to scare you."

The boy looked visibly relieved. Nonetheless, he quickly climbed out of the boat onto the sand and stood awkwardly facing Emma. Then as if he remembered something important, he stepped abruptly towards her and announced, "I'm Will."

"Nice to meet you, Will," Emma replied, extending her hand in his direction. "I'm Emma."

Will smiled shyly, then reached out and shook her hand.

188

Just then a voice from down the beach called out anxiously, "Will! Will Davies! Come here this instant."

"That's my Mom," Will told Emma apologetically as they both watched the woman make her way towards them.

"I'm not supposed to play over here," he explained sadly.

Will's mother had now reached the rowboats lining the shore and smiled tiredly at Will and Emma.

"I'm so sorry," she said. "I've told him over and over that this is private property, and he just can't come over here whenever he wants and..."

"Please," Emma said, "it's really no problem. He's fine."

"I do have to admit," she added, "it was kind of nice to see him playing down here. It's been too long since anyone did, I think."

Will's mother smiled, then shrugged.

"I'm afraid he just loves it here," she said, looking around, "though I'm not really sure why. My cousins and I always used to sneak over here and swim with the kids who were staying in the cottages. Then, of course, the owners would always chase us away."

"That was probably the attraction for us," she went on laughing softly, "trying to play over here without getting caught...you know how kids are. But it's been deserted for so long, so I don't get why Will..."

"I love it here too," Emma interrupted, laying a reassuring hand on the woman's arm, then adding cheerfully, "which is actually why I just bought it."

"Bought it?" the woman exclaimed. "You just bought Standish Village?"

"Why yes," Emma replied, a little taken aback, she had to admit, by the woman's surprised reaction.

189

"I'm Emma, Emma Lakin," she persevered nonetheless, "the new owner."

Will's mother had now gathered her son into her arms and was staring at Emma suspiciously.

"And you are?" Emma ventured.

"Oh sorry," the woman replied, visibly embarrassed, "Karen …Karen Davies."

Then she paused, and sliding her hand away from her son's shoulder, she extended it in Emma's direction and smiled weakly.

"I'm sorry," she said, "It's just that the place has been empty for so long, I was, you know, surprised to hear it was suddenly sold."

"I live over there," Karen added pointing down the beach behind her. "It used to be my parents' house, but now it's mine…mine and Will's."

She looked down at her son affectionately, running her hand gently through his chaotic red curls.

"Well, I'll be living here soon, I hope," Emma said, "with my son, Luke."

Will looked up hopefully.

"Sorry," Emma told him. "He's fifteen."

"But a nice fifteen," she added, when she saw the disappointed look on the little boy's face.

"I guess I have a lot of work to do first, though," Emma went on, as both women now looked up the hill toward the group of cottages. "My cottage is all set, but I have to admit I'm a little afraid to look at the others."

"Maybe I could help you with that," Karen said, brightening. "I know a lot of people around here and I could probably give you the names of some who are looking for work."

"I mean, guys who are really good, but not as expensive as some others, maybe," she added.

"Truthfully," Karen went on, "one of them is a friend of my brother's...he's actually staying with us right now, and I know he would love to..."

"Thanks," Emma said, "but I've got this guy, Charlie, helping me right now, and another woman, her name is Alice? I think maybe I should see what they have in mind first."

"I kind of owe them," she added, "for a bunch of things they've already done, I mean...they were out here working all day today, in fact."

Karen glanced back up toward the cottages again, and then hesitated slightly.

"Today?" she said. "I didn't see anyone out here today. Except you, that is."

Emma studied her carefully.

"Well," she said, a bit too enthusiastically she felt later, "maybe you just didn't see them. They were working up by the cottages and everything..."

Karen nodded.

"I'm sure that's it," she said. "Anyhow, let me know if you need anything...like I said, we live right over there."

Then urgently tugging at her son's arm, she turned and hurried away down the beach pulling him along beside her.

By now that sun had slipped away behind the trees on the other side of the pond and a gentle breeze began to chill the air and ripple the water nearby. Emma pulled her sweatshirt tighter around her and started back up the hill toward the cluster of cottages, their darkened facades looming gloomily among the pines. Thankfully she had remembered to leave a light on inside cottage #9, and when she climbed the steps to the porch, its warm glow welcomed her home.

Home! Emma thought, as the front door squeaked open and she walked inside. She was surprised at how quickly she had come to call the cottage this, and yet it seemed as if it always was...her home that is...one that was carelessly abandoned years ago and now was happily restored. Switching on the lamps as she went from room to room, Emma was soon enveloped by the comfort and security of the cottage.

Then, wandering into the tiny office, she sat down in the swivel chair, reached over and picked up the phone. Once again, the reassuring dial tone buzzed in her ear. Emma punched in her brother, Joel's phone number and waited for it to ring on the other end.

"Hey Mom," Luke said as soon as he picked up. "How's it goin' out there?"

"How did you know it was me?" Emma exclaimed.

"I have special powers," Luke replied laughing. "Plus, Uncle Joel has caller ID, and who else would be calling here from Unknown, Chatham, Massachusetts?"

"And," he added, "my Mom radar went off a few minutes ago...as in, it was just about time for you to call and check up on me...make sure I'm fulfilling my babysitting duties properly."

A loud clatter in the background, followed by several cheerful shrieks and giggles echoed through the phone line.

"What was that?" Emma demanded.

"Oh nothing," Luke said. This was followed by the unmistakable sound of his hand quickly covering the mouth of the receiver and a few muffled words.

"The little girls and I are making cookies!" he announced cheerfully, returning to the phone.

"Do you even know how to make cookies?" Emma asked.

"How hard can it be?" Luke said. Emma could just visualize him grinning and shrugging his shoulders, and was seized with a sudden pang of loneliness.

"Well, just don't burn the house down," Emma said, in what she thought was her stern mom voice. "that would not be beneficial for my sibling relationships.

"So anyways," Luke said, a slight hint of annoyance in his voice. "How are things on the Cape?"

"Great!" Emma replied, perhaps a bit too enthusiastically, she immediately thought. "I mean, so far, so good. You should see our cottage!"

"Of course, you didn't see it before," she added, "so maybe you wouldn't notice ...or appreciate...the, uh, difference."

There was silence on the other end of the line.

"*Our* cottage?" Luke asked finally.

"Um...yes...you know, the one I stayed in with my family when I was a kid?" Emma said. "The one I thought that we...you and I...might, um, use?"

"Oh," Luke said. "Sure, of course, that one. What about it?"

Emma could tell Luke was still trying to work up some enthusiasm for the conversation, but continued nonetheless.

"Completely modernized," she said. "All new furnishings, a second bathroom, even a fancy new stove."

"Oh yeah?" Luke teased. "And what could you possibly use that for?"

And he's back, Emma thought. Same old Luke she knew and adored.

"Luke," she began hesitantly, "I really called to ask you something."

"The answer's no, Mom," Luke joked, "I haven't started doing drugs. But I may consider it, if you ask me again."

"That's not what I was going to ask," Emma retorted.

"Okay, then what?" Luke asked.

"Remember when we were out here a few weeks ago," Emma began, "and you said something to me about Standish Village being haunted?"

"Haunted? You mean like ghosts running around and stuff?"

"Well, not exactly running around," Emma said, "just, you know, existing."

"Sort of," Luke replied cautiously. "I mean I sort of remember suggesting something like that...why?"

"No reason," Emma hesitated again. "I guess I was just wondering, was there somewhere you heard that? Like when we were staying at the inn in town? Maybe when I wasn't there? What I'm asking is, did anyone there happen to mention that about Standish Village? It being haunted, I mean? Someone at the inn...or someplace else you were around town?"

"Mom," Luke said firmly, "I was just kidding when I said that. I mean, I don't even remember saying it. And if I did, it was probably just

194

some spoiled brat kid thing, because I didn't want you to buy the place and then have to move there."

"But I told you," he added quickly, "I'm fine about it now. I'm all in, remember?"

"Ghosts or no ghosts!" he declared.

Just then, a little girl squeal sounded again in the background.

"Uh, oh!" Luke remarked nervously. "Ashley that's too much flour! Mom, I gotta go! Let's talk more later, okay?"

"Don't forget to clean that up. Missy will have a fit if you don't, and use..." Emma shouted into the receiver. There was an abrupt click and the line went dead.

"...the dustbuster." Emma told the dial tone.

"Because flour is impossible to sweep up," she added to no one, gently replacing the receiver on its hook. The she turned and stared out through the little window at the quickly descending darkness. For a brief moment, she thought she saw a small brown bird chirping merrily, as he hopped through the branches of the shadowy scrub pine still growing there.

Erni Johnson

Chapter Twenty: Ghost Stories (1975)

The summer Emma was 10 was the first time that she and Skip went to one of the bonfires on the Standish Village beach; though if the truth be known, they weren't actually invited...the bonfires were mostly created for the teenagers, who wanted to escape from the little family cottage at night (and also for their parents who were all too happy to have them do so). That particular evening, Emma and Skip, having both told their parents they were going to the other one's cottage to play board games, instead crept down the darkened path leading to the pond, and hid behind the row of bushes that lined the shore. There, sitting on the ground back to back, leaning against each other for support, they listened to the teenage talk and laughter drifting across the sand.

There were 10 of them that August...teenagers, that is: Emma's brothers, two of Skip's older sisters (the youngest of the three being not quite 13 and shunned by the older ones that year), as well another boy and his sister (she, rumored to have a terrible crush on Joel) and oddly enough, two sets of 15 year-old twins (one male pair, and one female pair) who were cousins, the offspring of identical female twins as well. Emma always thought Stephen had a thing for one of the girl twins, not learning until years later that his real "HT" that summer was, in fact, one of the boys.

With the exception of one other 12 year-old girl (a shy, only child who Skip's abandoned sister no doubt befriended out of sheer desperation), the other children in the Village that year were mostly toddlers, whose young parents found the tamer waters of White Pond preferable to the hearty waves of the oceanside resorts; children who were also put to bed hours earlier. Thus, the chances of Emma and Skip being discovered in their leafy hideout was minimal.

As the logs on the nearby bonfire crackled and burned, Emma secretly hoped that the brief silences in the teenage chatter might mean someone was kissing, but she didn't want to mention this to Skip who, having less romantic interests, had confided in her that he suspected the group might be smoking cigarettes and possibly even be drinking beer!

"How would you know that?" Emma demanded in a quiet whisper. She was, of course, disappointed that this was all the information Skip had come up with from his sisters, but then, as her mother once told her, boys forget to be romantic if you don't remind them they're supposed to be. Emma suspected her mother was referring to her father at that moment, but still considered it to be good advice to store away for the future.

Skip shrugged, which, (because Emma couldn't see him in the darkness), she only knew when she felt his shoulders twitch against hers.

"Because one time I found a package of cigarettes in Anna's beach bag," he said, then added proudly, "and she paid me a dollar not to tell Mom."

"I don't think my brothers smoke," Emma replied uncertainly, "and my parents would kill Joel if they found out he drank beer."

She actually didn't know for a fact that this was true, but the superior tone Skip used when he revealed the scandalous cigarette discovery, was enough to make Emma feel she had to have her own inside information on her siblings' behavior. As it turned out, it was a more than effective ploy.

"He drinks beer!" Skip exclaimed in what could only be described as a louder than average stage whisper.

"Shhhh..." Emma said, as she sat upright and turned slightly in Skip's direction. "Do you want to get caught?"

"What was that?" one of the girls at the bonfire demanded.

"What was what?" Emma heard her brother, Stephen respond calmly.

"That noise," the girl insisted. "Sounded sort of like whispering."

"Oh, that was probably just the ghosts!" one of the boy twins teased.

"Yeah," added the other, an eerie inflection in his voice. "The Ghosts of Standish Village! This is about the time they come out every night, right Joel?"

Emma could hear Skip's sister, Eleanor, start to giggle nervously, followed by the sound of what was probably the first girl slapping Joel on the arm.

"Oh right," the girl said. "There aren't any ghosts here."

"Oh no?" One of the boy twins replied. "Joel, tell these sweet little things about the old painter who comes back looking for his paint and brushes!"

"And the lady who keeps trying to find her kid who drowned in the pond!" his brother chimed in.

"Or how about the old lady who comes back in the middle of the night and starts vacuuming all the cottages?" Emma heard Stephen suggest; no doubt wanting to assert his own knowledge of Standish Village ghost sightings, she assumed.

"The one that leaves homemade pies baking in the ovens?" One of the girls asked. "My mom says sometimes she can smell one cooking, but when she gets up and looks in the oven there's nothing there."

"Well, my dad once woke up in the middle of the night and heard her cleaning the cottage next door, but when he looked over there it was all dark!" Stephen asserted firmly, no doubt, Emma imagined, turning towards his older brother for confirmation.

"Nah," Joel stated brusquely. "I wouldn't want to scare all these little ladies."

"Oh, like we'd be scared of a stupid old ghost story," Skip's sister, Anna remarked haughtily. "Pul-lease!"

"Yeah, gimme a break!'" the other girl twin scoffed.

"Okay then, here goes," Joel said in a deep serious voice. "You asked for it, don't forget."

Then he cleared his throat and began.

"Once, a long time ago, before any of us were born, even, there was this painter guy that the new owner of Standish Village hired to repaint the cottages," he explained.

"You see, the cottages were all sort of rundown and empty back then, because all the owners died or moved away or something...I forget what..." Joel went on "and the place just sort of sat here for years and years before this new owner decide to buy it."

"It was because of the Great Depression," Stephen interrupted, in an authoritarian tone. "Before that, the cottages were all owned by rich people from Boston, and when they lost all their money in the

Stock Market Crash of 1929, they never came back to the Cape, and the cottages were just abandoned."

"Yeah, whatever," Joel said, clearly annoyed at Stephen's intrusion. "So...as I was saying, the cottages were all empty and this guy bought them really cheap, and then he hired another guy, a painter, to come and put a fresh coat of paint on them so he could sell them at a big profit."

"One of the guys that owned a cottage here actually killed himself...jumped off a building in Boston when he found out all his money was gone," Stephen said.

At this point, Emma could just picture Joel glaring at Stephen before continuing his narrative.

"ANY-way," Joel said firmly, "the owner, the guy who bought the place, I mean, waited until the painter guy had repainted all the cottages and they looked really nice, and then told him that he didn't like how he had done the work and fired him."

"So, then what happened?" the first girl twin asked. "And what about the part about the ghost?"

"Hold on!" Joel declared. "I'm getting to that."

"What happened was, that the owner made the painter leave the property right then, right when he fired him...I heard he even aimed a gun at him..." Here Joel paused for dramatic effect.

"...because he figured, you know, the painter guy might take his painting tools, scrapers and hammers and stuff, and wreck everything he did," he explained.

"But the painter," he went on, "snuck back in that night to get all his equipment."

"And then did he wreck the cottages?" Emma heard Eleanor ask.

"Of course not!" Joel exclaimed. "You see, the painter guy was a real craftsman...someone who was really proud of his work, and couldn't wait for people to buy the cottages and admire what he had done. He was even thinking if he could earn enough money he would buy one himself, because he always wanted to live right here!"

Several teenagers groaned at this.

"Was he nuts?!" one declared. "Always wanted to live on this lame little pond?"

Several other kids murmured in hearty agreement.

"But what about the ghost?!" the same girl twin insisted. "When are you going to tell us that part of the story?!"

"So..." Joel went on, a bit annoyed, Emma noticed. "All the painter wanted to do..."

Both Emma and Skip leaned toward the bushes at this point, as Joel's voice softened (and no doubt, the other teenagers at the bonfire leaned toward him as well).

"...was pick up his stuff," Joel continued, "and move on to his next job."

"But when he snuck back into the property," Joel said, his voice building dramatically, "THERE was the owner with his shotgun ...aimed...directly...at...the ...carpenter's...head...and...BANG!"

The girls (and possibly some of the guys as well, Emma thought later), shrieked.

"He killed him???" Eleanor cried. "The owner killed the painter??"

"Yup," Joel said solemnly, "and the rumor is that he tied a cement block to the painter's feet, put him in one of these boats..."

Emma could just picture Joel gesturing to one of the decaying wooden rowboats pulled up on the beach.

"...then rowed to the middle of the pond, and dropped the painter's body into the water," Joel concluded.

There was a brief silence as Joel's audience absorbed the horror of the tale; meanwhile, the bonfire snapped and crackled loudly and small sparks floated over the bushes behind which Emma and Skip were hiding.

"So, you're saying the painter...his ghost...comes back every night, looking for his paint and brushes and stuff," one the boy twins inquired uneasily, his former bravado apparently gone now.

"I'm not 'saying' he does," Joel replied, "I'm telling you that he does."

"And what?" Emma heard Anna remark sarcastically, "tries to kill everyone staying here? Or has he decided to wreck all the cottages after all. My dad was just saying how they seem to be falling apart more every year."

"Of course not!" Joel scoffed. "The painter loves this place. In fact, he just sneaks around and tries to paint things, while he looks for the rest of his equipment."

"So how is that scary?" Anna asked. "Sounds like he's a friendly ghost."

"Well," Joel replied casually, "he only hurts people who try to mess things up...you know like those teenagers at the bonfires who smoke and drink beer?"

This last comment was followed by gales of male laughter and sounds of obvious female disgust.

"But what about the vacuuming lady?" One of the girl twins asked, after the hilarity had subsided, "the one who bakes pies in all the cottage ovens?

"Or the one who comes back looking for her son who drowned?" her sister pleaded. "Is she a friendly ghost too?"

Emma heard Stephen scoff.

"I wouldn't think she'd be especially friendly, the lady whose kid drowned, I mean," he said, "especially if it was someone else who let him drown...she'd be out for vengeance."

"I don't think that's true, Stephen," Eleanor said. "I mean think about it, she'd be so sad...desperate maybe, even. Trying to make friends with everyone she met and get them to help her find her little boy!"

"Is that what her ghost does, Joel?" She asked.

There was a silence during which Emma could imagine Joel mustering up his most serious expression.

"As a matter of fact," Joel said at last, "that's actually a much scarier story..."

It was at this point, Emma now recalled, as she lay in bed in cottage #9, as the current new owner of Standish Village, that Skip suddenly scrambled to his feet and grabbing her hand dragged her with him out of their hiding spot and back onto the path leading to the cottages.

"Let's go, Emma," he had whispered frantically.

"But..." Emma began, as a part of her wanted to stay and listen to the next story. Nonetheless, she had followed her friend back up the hill away from the laughing teenagers and the still glowing bonfire, because it did seem like what she'd really wanted to do at the time. But now, as she lay there in the dark, the moon casting an insistent glow across the end of her bed, she suddenly wished she had stayed.

Chapter Twenty-One: Progress (2003)

When Emma awoke the next morning, it was to the sound of hammering somewhere nearby, and the screech and rattle of an extension ladder opening and then banging decidedly on the side of the cottage next door. Good old Charlie, Emma thought, up at the crack of dawn and back to work. Then she rolled over and squinted at the clock on her bedside table. Nine o'clock? How could that be? When she had fully intended to be up and dressed hours ago!

Oh well, it was Saturday, after all, and even though Emma planned to spend the day fixing up her new cottage (and assessing the needs of the other ones, of course), it seemed as if her new friends had beat her to it, at least in terms of the initial task. She leaned back on her pillows and gazed happily around the room. The crisp, clear morning breeze rustled the curtains at the open windows and soft rays of gentle sunlight slid across the quilt and danced in the mirror of the white wooden vanity. Suddenly last night's dreams of ghosts and haunted cottages faded away in the glory of a warm spring morning on Cape Cod.

It was then that Emma smelled it: the unmistakable aroma of fresh brewed coffee. Reaching for the sweatpants at the end of her bed, she swung her legs out from under the covers and hastily pulled them on under the oversized tee shirt in which she'd fallen asleep. Then she grabbed last night's abandoned sweatshirt from a nearby chair, and yanking it carelessly over her head, she wandered barefoot down the hall and into the kitchen.

Sure enough, steaming happily in a coffee maker perched on the counter was a pot of fresh brewed coffee. On the breakfast table across the room sat a mug, plate, juice glass, and carefully folded napkin. Next to these was a small cardboard bakery box tied with a thin, white string, which Emma immediately cut with a knife she found lying next to it. Inside were two fresh cinnamon rolls, their sugary glaze reflecting the morning sun as it streamed in through the windows on the porch.

"Who would have..." Emma began (speaking to the emptiness of her kitchen). But then she knew: Alice, of course. Suddenly she was famished and walking back to the counter, she poured herself a steaming hot cup of coffee, grabbed the juice bottle from the refrigerator, and sat down at the table ready to dig in. The sticky edge of the bun clung to her fingers as she lifted it to her mouth and took a bite. Perfect! She thought, as the sweetness of the pastry lay happily in her mouth and welcomed her to the day ahead.

Still, even amid the sugary breakfast contentment, Emma could not shake the uneasy feeling that something was just not right; the rundown plaza with the deserted Parker Real Estate office, Charlie and Alice appearing exactly when and where she needed their supportive gestures; and the way cottage #9 was perfectly renovated and waiting for her, before she even signed the final sale papers, and only days after she'd casually suggested to Ted Parker that she might want to stay here this weekend.

And then there was Luke's offhand comment about Standish Village being haunted, one that had, no doubt, prompted last night's sudden memory of that time she and Skip spied on the teenagers' bonfire and listened to Joel's ghost stories; something she hadn't thought about in years and in fact, had pretty much forgotten. Now she was even dreaming about it, for god's sake.

Oh, don't be ridiculous, Emma told herself, as she polished off the last cinnamon roll and wiped the final scraps of sticky icing from the corner of her mouth. Just because Standish Village sat on the market for years didn't mean there was anything wrong with it...much less that it was haunted. It was simply that the right buyer hadn't come along. After all, at any given time, there were plenty of properties up for sale in a tourist area like this. Potential investors had their pick, as it were, and it was just a question of individual taste.

Maybe a nice, hot shower would help clear her head, Emma decided, as she carried her breakfast dishes to the sink. But as she headed down the hall towards her bedroom, she glanced through the doorway of the tiny office and noticed the light on the answering machine blinking steadily. Now that's odd, she thought, I don't remember the phone ringing earlier. Could I have been that sound asleep, she wondered? Emma entered the little room, walked over to the desk and pushed the message button on the machine.

"Hello?" the recording began, "Emma? Ted Parker here. I guess you haven't recorded your outgoing message yet, because I got the canned one, but I'm pretty sure this is the right number."

Then there was a pause as if, Emma observed, Ted Parker was expecting some sort of response at this juncture.

"Well, anyway," he went on at last. "I just wanted to let you know that a while back...before you decided to buy Standish Village...in fact, before you even came to look at the place..."

At this point, Ted Parker chuckled slightly.

"Come to think of it, those two occasions were quite close together and both quite recent, so maybe it wasn't that long ago..." he continued. "But my point is, I went and hired some folks...handyman types, I guess you'd call 'em...to do a little bit a' renovation, I guess you might say. You know, fix the cottages up a bit, so the place would be...a little more...saleable?"

Wasn't there a time limit on this machine? Emma wondered at this point. But Ted Parker was still talking.

"So, the thing is," he was saying. "I didn't get around to cancelling these guys...you know, telling them the place was sold and whatnot, and well...uh...Charlie called and said they came to work this mornin'."

Another pause followed this revelation.

"I'll pay for whatever they've done so far, naturally," Ted Parker added quickly, "and if you don't like it, you can..."

Mercifully, at this point, the answering machine seemed to have reached its limit and with a high pitched beep, the message stopped, and the light vanished. Emma stood staring at it for a few moments, then turned and walked out of the office. As she stepped into her tiny new tile shower, she smiled. What the heck? As long as the work gets done right? Then she turned on the water and let it run reassuringly over her face and arms, filling the air and fogging the mirror over the miniature sink with a comforting cloud of steam.

Later that morning, after she'd dressed and had another cup of coffee on the porch, Emma put on her sneakers and ventured out into the Village to check on the progress of Ted Parker's reported renovations. Sure enough, the first thing Emma saw was Charlie high up on a ladder painting a newly scrapped surface on the cottage next door.

"Hey there!" she called up to him. "How's it going?"

Charlie peered down through the rungs of the ladder, dangling a dripping paint brush from his hand.

"Emma!" he declared. "So nice to see ya! Lovely mornin' ain't it?"

"Can I get you some coffee?' Emma offered. "Alice left a whole pot brewing in my kitchen, and if I drink all that I'll be awake for the next four days!"

Charlie chuckled.

"That'd be Alice, all right," he said. "She was here even earlier than me this mornin'. Already cleanin' and scrubbin'."

Charlie nodded his head on the general direction of the line of cottages from which Emma could hear the faint drone of a vacuum cleaner.

"But I'll pass on the coffee," Charlie added, pointing to a thermos sitting on the ground at the bottom of his ladder. "Had me more an' enough already, I suspect."

"Okay," Emma replied, "but if you change your mind, just let me know."

Charlie nodded and went back to his painting, and Emma started down the path toward the pond, but then abruptly she stopped.

"Say, Charlie," she said, "I got a call from Ted this morning...something about hiring some guys to help out..."

"Oh yeah, yeah," Charlie replied, "I almost forgot. A few of those guys showed up and I had 'em do some scraping and siding repairs and whatnot."

"It was definitely a help," he added, "but I think we can take it from here. Told Ted that, in fact. That is, if it's okay with you..."

"Oh, I totally agree," Emma said firmly. "I may not look like a carpenter, but I learned a lot from my dad over the years and I'm sure I can pitch in!"

Charlie looked down at her silently and then rubbed his chin thoughtfully.

"I'm sure you can," he remarked cautiously, "but you know, also we got that fella come over from next door...you know, the red-haired guy. The one Ted told ya come around the other day."

Charlie removed his painter's hat and ran his hand through his bushy white hair before repositioning it back on his head.

"Man," he declared, "he's one heck of a good worker. It's like he's got some personal stake in the place, the way he goes at the repairs and whatnot. That was a smart move you made takin' on that fella!"

"But I..." Emma began, then realized that maybe she didn't want to admit to Charlie that her brother, Joel, had undoubtedly hired this guy because he thought Emma was too helpless to handle things herself.

"I'm glad he's working out," she said, then looking around, she added, "where is he anyhow? I'd like to intro...I mean, say hello...you know...see how he's getting on."

Charlie looked out from his perch on the top of the ladder.

"Huh," he said, turning his head slowly in different directions, "dunno. He was down by the shuffleboard and whatnot a bit ago, but not sure right now."

Charlie shrugged. "If I see him, I'll be sure and let 'im know you was lookin' for him."

"Thanks," Emma replied, but Charlie just nodded, grinned again, and went back to his painting, and Emma continued her walk towards the pond.

When she reached the grassy area where the shuffleboard and croquet shed had stood worn and neglected just a few weeks earlier, Emma was startled by the change that had taken place in the interim. The shuffleboard court, its lines and point designations once faded by sun and constant competition, was now freshly painted and ready for new challenges. The croquet shed, which earlier that spring leaned to one side precariously, its little door sagging sadly on broken hinges, was now upright, and painted a bright red. And when Emma gently opened the miniature door on its shiny new hinges, a row of solid new mallets greeted her, along with a bucket of matching wooden balls and an organized row of aluminum wickets.

Even the basketball court on the other side of the newly raked lawn boasted sharp new lines, the grass along its paved edges was neatly trimmed, and a crisp, white net now hung from a no longer rusted metal hoop. It seemed that the only area still neglected was a sad patch of dirt on the far side of the game area, one that apparently, as Emma drew closer and examined it carefully, had once been a garden. Well, she thought, this is as good a place to start as any. It was spring, after all, and with the day growing steadily warmer, why not plant a garden!

By late afternoon, Emma had been to the nursery where she bought gardening gloves, a hoe, shovel, and a few bags of soil, plus a selection of hardy perennials. Then she struggled with weeds and rocks until the surface of the garden was at least somewhat ready for the new plants, but as the daylight began to fade, Emma made the decision that tomorrow would be planting day.

Standish Village was quiet and peaceful as Emma trudged back up the hill to her cottage. There was no sign of either Charlie or Alice, but the spotlights gently glowing from the line of cottages was a reassuring sign of their earlier presence, and Emma found herself oddly content in her evening solitude. Nor was she surprised, once she was back inside Cottage #9, to find a chicken casserole waiting on the counter, along with a carefully written set of instructions on how to prepare it.

Just as she popped it into the oven, however, there was a soft knocking on the porch door.

"Hello?" Emma called, as she closed the oven, and tossed the oven mitts on the counter. "Who's there?"

"It's me," a female voice answered. "Karen. Karen Davies, from next door? We met earlier when my son was...well... trespassing?"

Then she laughed. By now, Emma had reached the front door and through the screen, standing in a haze of moths and other flying bugs drawn to the porch light, she saw the woman she met earlier on the beach.

"Oh hi!" Emma exclaimed. "Come in!"

"Um, you might want to hit that light first," Karen remarked, swatting casually at the buzzing insects, "unless you also want to entertain all these creatures."

"Of course," Emma said, reaching for the switch. "Sorry."

Then, as the nighttime insect noise slowly ceased, Emma opened the door slightly and Karen slipped in, pulling it quickly closed behind her.

"Sorry," Emma said, "I guess I'm not used to country living quite yet."

"Country, plus seaside," Karen added. "Makes for an interesting evening combination."

"And by the way," Emma said, as she moved toward the kitchen, "your son was not trespassing! In fact, it was nice to see a kid playing down by the pond after all these years."

"Okay, if you say so...personally I enjoyed the break. He can be a handful sometimes," Karen said, and then extended her hand in which she held a bottle of wine. "I brought this. Wanna share?"

"Absolutely," Emma replied, taking the offered bottle. "I think that's the perfect vintage to go with the chicken casserole in my oven."

"Oh my god, you cooked?" Karen declared as she strode into the kitchen and leaned down to peer through the glass oven door. "I thought you spent the whole afternoon working on that old garden."

Then she quickly straightened and gasped slightly with embarrassment.

"I mean, it's not like I was spying on you or anything..." she began.

"But you were," Emma said, then both women laughed.

"Okay," Karen said, "maybe I was a little. But only because I thought it was so cool you were restoring that old garden. It used to be so beautiful...just bursting with blooms!"

"I know!" Emma said. "I remember it so well!"

"Remember it?" Karen asked.

"Yes," Emma replied, as she opened the drawer next to the stove and retrieved what appeared to be a brand new cork screw.

"My parents used to bring us...my brothers and me...to Standish Village when I was a kid," she explained, as she reached up and opened a nearby cupboard. Could there actually be wine glasses somewhere as well? Yup, there they were, all right, just sitting on the first shelf, waiting for her to find them. She removed two and set them on the counter.

"I was much younger than my brothers," Emma went on as she uncorked the wine and carried the bottle and glasses to the table where Karen now sat. "So, when they all started playing croquet, or basketball or whatever, I usually just ended up watching. I guess that's why I remember the garden...when I got bored, I used to walk around the paths and watch the butterflies and, I confess, pick flowers for our cottage."

"This cottage," she added, waving her hand in the general direction of the rest of the dwelling.

"Really?" Karen exclaimed. "This was the cottage you stayed in with your family?"

"Yup," Emma said, as she sat down across from her new friend. "We came here every July for five or six years...until one night my older brother decided to get drunk and smashed up the family car."

"Seriously?" Karen exclaimed. "Did he get hurt?"

"No, no," Emma replied, shaking her head. "just a little gash over his eye. The car got the worst of it. But my parents were truly pissed and we left for home the next day."

"Never to return!" she declared, raising her wine glass in a theatrical toast."

"I expect my parents were more embarrassed than anything else," she added. "You know, all those summer people with the perfect kids. Of course, little did they know that a bunch of their little sweethearts were in the car with brother sharing that beer."

"And their parents never found out?" Karen asked.

"Well, not from Joel at least," Emma said. "My big brother may be a dope about a lot of things, but if nothing else, he's very loyal...and way too protective. Both my brothers are. You'd think I was still some little kid the way they treat me...geez."

Karen smiled.

"I know what you mean," she said. "I come from a big family...siblings, cousins, aunts, and uncles galore, and they were *always* fussing over me and warning me about all the *dangers* of life, even after I was grown up and had a kid of my own. Probably because I was the youngest...but that didn't make it any less annoying."

"Are they still that way?" Emma asked. "Over-protective, I mean?"

Karen sighed.

"Not really, I guess," she said. "I mean, I don't actually see them much anymore. We all used to come out here in the summer, the whole huge family, and stay in the big house where Will and I live now. But then, I don't know, things changed...the kids grew up, got married, moved away, and with the older generation gone now too, well, you know how it goes..."

Emma nodded.

"My parents are gone too," she said, "and my brothers have their own lives. I know they still care about me, but most of the time it's just me and Luke, and even he's getting pretty grown up."

Emma looked around the room in which the two women sat. "I guess that's why it felt so good coming back here. Like it was a piece of my life I didn't quite finish... you know, because we never came back after that last summer; like a time that seems sort of idyllic. Maybe I just want that kind of innocent happiness again."

"Exactly how I felt when I came back here to live with Will," Karen agreed. "I suppose I could have sold the house after my parents died, but it seemed like I had something to finish as well...or maybe I wanted to share how it felt for me with Will...that piece of my childhood, I mean."

"Despite all the 'protection'," she added, grinning mischievously, as she made air quotes with her fingers.

"Of course, Cottage #9 did look a bit different in those days." Emma confessed, as she topped off their glasses of wine. "You might go as far as to say it was pretty rustic back in the 70s."

Then she smiled.

"Not that I'm sorry Ted got it all fixed up for me," she continued, "and Charlie and Alice have been wonderful too...it's like they're still trying to convince me to buy the place when I already did! Or at least convince me to stay...that I made the right choice, that is."

"Charlie and Alice?" Karen inquired.

"Yes," Emma replied eagerly. "Such nice people. I just met them and already they've done so much for me. Alice even made this casserole, and Charlie, he's the one I mentioned before who was out all day painting. The guy has to be at least 70 and he's already repainted three or four cottages."

Karen eyed her cautiously.

"Are they local?" she asked.

"Yup," Emma said. "I mean I assume they're even long time locals. Charlie told me he used to be in the town band back in the 70s, and Alice...I'm guessing she runs a bakeshop or something...in addition to the storage facility where all the cottage stuff was stored."

"And she's no spring chicken either," Emma added, as she emptied her glass and reached across the table for the bottle.

"You'll have to introduce me," Karen said, "especially to Alice. That casserole smells delicious. And we haven't had a decent bakery in this town for years. I can't wait to try hers!"

"And who's Ted?" she asked sipping her wine.

"Ted Parker," Emma replied. "The guy who owns the real estate agency? The company that was listing this place? You know him?"

"Hmmm...not sure..." Karen remarked thoughtfully, then added, "oh yeah, sure, I remember him...didn't he have an office down in that plaza where the laundromat used to be? I didn't realize he was still around...you know, after the accident and all?"

"Accident?" Emma asked.

"Right," Karen said. "The boat accident...the one where Gordy Anderson...um..."

"Oh," Emma interrupted quickly. "Yes, I heard about that. I mean I didn't know Gordy, I just heard that was why Standish Village was on the market...how Gordy was starting to fix it up as condos and everything and then...the accident happened. So tragic huh?"

"Yes, it was," Karen said, swirling the wine in her glass and then taking another sip, as she gazed out the kitchen window toward the pond.

"But what does that have to do with Ted?" Emma asked cautiously. "were they good friends?"

Karen turned to look at Emma in surprise.

"Why yes," she said, then paused.

"It was Ted's boat," she added. "I'm sorry, I thought you knew."

An hour or so later, the chicken casserole (as well as another bottle of wine) consumed, the two women wandered out to the porch and leaned back in the cushioned wicker chairs, the lighthouse candle on the glass-topped table gently glowing between them. Standish Village was dark now, but through the trees, the surface of the pond was softly lit by the moon, and the insistent chirp of the peepers nearby filled the night air.

"So, are you here for good?" Karen asked. "I'm just thinking I could easily do this again…as long as the wine holds out, that is, and those casseroles keep mysteriously appearing."

Emma nodded.

"I could too," she said, "but sadly I'll be heading back home tomorrow. I still have a school year to finish and a son to feed."

"Lord knows what kind of junk he's been scoffing down while I was gone," she added.

"Oh, you're a teacher?" Karen inquired.

"Just until the end of the year," Emma declared firmly. "Then I plan to be an innkeeper, or a village keeper, or whatever running this place is called."

"Big step," Karen observed, as she turned to study her companion.

"Yeah, I know," Emma said. "But I feel like it's time I need to move forward. My friend, Skip always used to tell me I didn't do enough of that...moving forward, I mean. That I just sort of sat there and dealt with whatever anyone wanted to dump on me."

"Whew," Karen said, "that's a little harsh."

"Well," Emma replied, "I can't say he was totally wrong. I did sort of tend to let things happen to me rather than make them happen...and he has always been just the opposite."

"In fact," she added, "buying Standish Village might be the first thing I ever actually made happen...although Skip did have a lot to do with it."

"How so?" Karen asked.

"This is where we met...every summer his family always stayed right over there at the same time my family stayed here," Emma explained, gesturing toward the cottage next door. "We were the same age and our siblings much older, so we kind of got thrown together, and...you know...stayed friends."

"Where is he now?" Karen asked.

"Oh, who knows?" Emma said. "He travels a lot for his job. He's married too...might even have kids, for all I know...I hear from him once in a while, though...we were pen pals when we were kids."

Then she laughed.

"Sorry that sounds sort of lame, huh? It does seem a little silly now, but it was fun back then," she said. "Maybe more than fun...I mean, I always felt like he was the only one who really understood me...knew who I was...even though we didn't see each other much."

"Did I say he's the one who told me Standish Village was for sale?" Emma added, leaning forward in her chair. "In his Christmas card actually, and for some reason, that just made want to buy the place..."

Suddenly, when Emma actually said it out loud, the whole situation seemed rather absurd, and she found herself wondering if Karen's silence might be proof that it was.

"Well," Karen said at last, "I suppose that's as good a reason as any."

Then she sighed.

"I guess I have spent so many years on my own," Karen went on, "that it seems like having a friend like that would be something so special...certainly enough to inspire changing your life."

"You're very lucky to have him," she added, "wherever he might be."

Then she stood and pulled on the sweatshirt she'd tossed on the back of her chair earlier.

"I guess I should stagger my way home," she said, "I want to be there in time to tuck Will into bed."

Emma stood as well.

"Of course," she said. "Who's taking care of him tonight, anyhow?"

"Oh, just an old friend," Karen answered vaguely. "Someone I knew back when we lived in New Jersey...our families used to be close and well, he's been through some tough times lately, so, you know, I'm trying to help him get back on his feet, find a job, and what not. He's been staying with me for a couple weeks."

"He's great with kids," she added. "And luckily for me, Will adores him, or I wouldn't have had this night out!"

"We'll have to do it again," Emma said.

"And by the way," she called, as Karen headed down the cottage steps to the path below. "If your friend wants to do some work over here, I'd be happy to hire him."

Karen looked confused.

"Oh!" She said, obviously surprised by the offer, "I thought you already did."

Then she shrugged.

"I must have heard it wrong...when he told me he got a job, that is."

"But I'll tell him," she added, and disappeared into the night.

Chapter Twenty-Two: Dreams and Ambitions

"Did you ever wish you could just go back and start over?" Skip wrote to Emma the summer before they both went away to college. At the time, Emma thought this was a rather odd question to be asking right then, because wasn't going to college a sort of starting over thing anyhow?

Joel, whose college career, or basically lack thereof, was practically a decade in his past, was all too eager to offer Emma the advice he failed to follow himself.

"Take full advantage of these years," he told her, "while you're still secure in the knowledge that someone else is paying for your potential success. You'll never get another chance to prepare yourself for the future."

Of course, then he launched into another tale of fraternity escapades before he then headed off to his current job, which he claimed paid "twice as much as any of my friends with college degrees make."

Stephen hadn't been much more encouraging.

"College is just practice for graduate school," he told Emma on the phone. (At the time, he was wallowing in self-pity over "impossible graduate courses and ridiculous debt" in his studio apartment in the Bronx.)

Then he added glumly, "and I have no idea what graduate school is practice for."

But start over? What would be the point of that? Learning to ride a bike sooner so the other kids wouldn't make fun of her? Not getting the super short haircut in eighth grade? Not sending that "anonymous" love letter to Henry Carter (not like everyone didn't know who it was from). Better she should head off to college and reinvent a new self where no one knew the first thing about her embarrassing past than to go through all that again.

She was tempted to tell Skip exactly that...or better still, to even remind him that his sports star, honor student, friend-saturated childhood did not even need reinvention.

But she didn't. Instead, she asked him if he did start over...what exactly he would change?

"Well, I wouldn't change us," he wrote back, "and especially the time we spent together on 'that old Cape Cod.' Except maybe to make it last longer...maybe I'd move to Standish Village even, and live there all the time forever."

Emma thought he was kidding, of course. Or maybe just being sentimental because he was leaving home. Maybe he was even a little afraid of going off to college where no one knew him, whereas she was looking forward to the prospect of that anonymity. Besides, at that point it had been years since they were summer best friends...she could hardly remember Standish Village, in fact, but based on the pictures of the cottage her parents dragged out from time to time, it sure didn't look like somewhere she actually wanted to live "forever."

There had been Anna's wedding of course, back when they were 15, but even then, they'd only spent a few days together, most of which were consumed by wedding events. As Emma recalled, Skip didn't even get to the Cape until after some Lacrosse party back home in New Jersey, and then what? They hung out together for an afternoon...and that short time on the beach during the wedding reception? Chances are that once Skip got to the Cape, and his sisters and parents were all wrapped up in wedding stuff, he was just bored...which was probably the only reason they spent even that much time together.

Besides, Skip's parents still had that house on the Cape...a big comfortable house with what they called a "carriage house" behind it, which, Skip had written her last fall, had an upstairs apartment his parents allowed him to live in during his whole senior year in high school...well, at least when they were out there on vacations and stuff. Talk about not wishing for a do-over! Who would give that up!

When she finally wrote back to Skip again, Emma had planned to give him a big pep talk about how college could be just like starting over, only in a little different way, and tell him to think how much better that would be than going back and doing the same old stupid little kids things again. She even planned to remind him of some of their super dumb summer escapades as prime examples of why moving forward was the way to go.

But instead, she just asked the question: "why would you want to go back and start all over, when you could accomplish the same thing by moving forward?"

She had patted herself on the back a bit after that, thinking she had phrased the whole thing so eloquently and how it made such perfect sense that even Skip wouldn't be able to argue with her contention; even though he was known for always debating everything to the point where everyone just gave up and agreed with him.

She hadn't counted on his response.

"Emma," he wrote, "you're a fine one to talk about moving forward. I've known you for almost 10 years and I've never seen you move anywhere without being pushed."

After that, Emma stopped writing to him altogether, though subconsciously she spent most of her freshman year trying to prove him wrong...but with relatively little success. Well now I have, Emma thought, as she drove down the Mass Pike towards home after her first weekend at Standish Village. Not only did I go ahead and buy a cottage colony after everyone I know discouraged me, but I bought the one where Skip told me he wanted to go back and live forever.

"So there, Skip Peterson!" She declared out loud, smacking the steering wheel as she did. "I dare you to tell me now that I don't know how to move forward."

The problem was, of course, that Skip wasn't there to hear her. Not only that, but she didn't even know where Skip was, or when she'd be able to tell him about her big move, and she couldn't shake the nagging feeling that she never would.

Chapter Twenty-Three: Ghosts and Whatnot

"So, explain this to me again," Stephen said. "This motel...or, sorry, cottage colony...you decided to buy on Cape Cod is becoming miraculously renovated in record time (and apparently mostly for free), by some kindly older people who you now suspect are actually ghosts."

"And..." he added, in a clearly sarcastic tone, Emma observed, "you believe that the reason they are doing this is because somehow they are trying to convince you that this is your true destiny...that it is something that is just 'meant to be' (at this point he raised his hands making 'air quotes') after our family stayed in a cottage there 20-some years ago...or something like that."

He was sitting at Emma's kitchen table nursing a beer, while Emma stood at the counter nearby, her back to her brother, slicing cucumbers for a salad.

"I'm not saying they're all ghosts," she protested, as she turned and scraped the cucumber slices into a bowl on the table. "There's this one very nice woman named Karen, who lives next door...on the other end of the beach, I mean. And she's about my age, I think, not much older."

"Also," she went on, "there's this other young guy...he's staying with Karen, I think she said...anyhow, I suspect Joel actually hired him to help without telling me. I haven't actually seen him, but the way

Charlie...he's the older painter guy...describes him, he sounds like...like...someone I used to know."

Emma looked up at Stephen and smiled sheepishly.

"Someone you used to know..." Stephen repeated, then shook his head.

"Emma," he said setting his beer bottle on the table in front of him, "I hope you haven't told too many people about this whole thing, especially if you're hoping someone will actually come and stay there when you open."

"Haven't told too many people about what?" Luke asked, as he came into the kitchen and peered into the refrigerator. "Do we have any soda, Mom?"

"In the door," Emma replied, as she carried the salad bowl back to the counter. "And don't eat anything, dinner's in a half hour."

Luke turned toward his mother and grinned.

"And you think somehow I won't be hungry enough to eat it? Should I decide to have something to eat now?" he said.

Then he popped the top on his soda can and sat down opposite his uncle.

"What are you hoping she hasn't told people, Uncle Stephen?" he demanded. "That Standish Village is most likely haunted, but it's okay because they are kind, friendly ghosts, who are helping her fix up the place out of the goodness of their hearts?"

"Wait," he added, with a dramatic pause, "do ghosts actually still have hearts?"

Stephen groaned and laid his head down on the table.

"Not you too!" he mumbled.

232

Emma joined them at the table, reached across the surface and patted Stephen's arm.

"I know it sounds strange," she said. "But if you were there, it wouldn't seem that way...to either of you, actually. I mean maybe these are all just genuinely nice people...it's not impossible that someone like exists, you know."

Stephen raised his head and stared silently at his sister.

"Oh and..." Luke said, taking a large gulp of his soda, "did I mention that the old lady ghost makes awesome blueberry pie?"

"Oh well then," Stephen grumbled, "that settles it. I simply must experience all this for myself."

"Well, there ya go," Luke exclaimed. "That's the answer!"

"Don't you see?" he went on, when the other two turned to him in confusion. "We should all just go out there together...the three of us...and Uncle Jim, too, of course, if he wants to come...out to Standish Village and, you know, see for ourselves. We could even help you renovate, Mom!"

Emma studied her son and her brother cautiously. Something in her wanted to point out that she wasn't altogether sure how much help either of them would be when it came to renovating, but it would be nice to have them there, nonetheless. Besides there was something about the eager expression on Luke's face (and perhaps even the resignation apparent on Stephen's), that made the plan seem worth a try.

"Okay," she said, as she stood and took the chicken breasts out of the refrigerator. "But no scaring my ghosts away! There's still a lot of work to be done, after all."

Later Emma wondered why she didn't mention that she thought the other guy working on Standish Village was her friend, Skip...well, maybe the red-haired guy that Charlie told her about wasn't Skip, but his description sure sounded like him. And Karen's sort of secretive attitude about the "friend of the family" who was staying with them? If it actually was Skip, and not some random guy Joel hired and sent out there, then it would be just like him to swear everyone to secrecy...to just start fixing up the place for Emma, but not letting her know he was doing it.

But why would he do that? They hadn't parted on the greatest of terms last time she saw him, which was how long ago? Nine or ten years? Okay, it wasn't like anything really happened...it was just that she never did tell him about Luke initially, and then when they hung out on the beach that time in Florida and Skip was all into meeting up the next day, didn't Emma just leave without telling him? Without even calling to explain?

She couldn't even remember what made her decide to do that. Something about leaving the piece of paper with his number in the hotel? Stephen would say she did it on purpose, but she didn't, right? It was just part of her chaotic personality to do something like that. And Skip must have known that too, because didn't he keep sending her postcards and Christmas cards, and wasn't he even the one who told her this place was for sale? No, he definitely didn't have any hard feelings.

Still, there was no point in telling Stephen (or even asking Joel) about the red-haired guy, because what if it wasn't Skip, and she was just creating some fantasy in her head, that...that what? That owning Standish Village wasn't just her destiny, but also his? Perhaps even theirs together? To make up for something they missed? For "lost chances?"

Now where did that come from? Startled by that phrase abruptly surfacing in her thoughts, Emma dropped the frypan she was washing into the sudsy sink water. She stared out the window in front of her, desperately trying to remember if it was something Skip once told her...or she once told him? But nothing came back to her. Then she shrugged, and lifting the soapy pan from the sink, rinsed it and dropped in in the drain board.

So, all the more reason not to share her suspicions with Stephen. If and when he and Luke came with her to the Cape, and if and when the red-haired worker showed up and if he was, in fact, Skip, Emma would simply act as shocked and surprised as everyone else. That is, if any of it actually happened at all.

"Mom?" Luke had materialized at her side.

"Huh?" Emma felt herself jump. "Oh Luke, sorry, you startled me."

"Well I don't know why," he declared. "I've been calling you for the last 10 minutes, and face it, Mom, it's not that big a house."

Emma smiled.

"Sorry," she said again, "I was just thinking about something."

"About what?" Luke asked.

"Oh, just that old Cape Cod," Emma said.

"Yeah, well, when you're done with that, could you help me find that old Lacrosse uniform I need for tomorrow's game?" Luke replied.

"Of course," Emma said, "it's got to be around here somewhere. You can always find what you're looking for if you try hard enough."

"I guess that's true," Luke replied and grinned.

Chapter Twenty-Four: Lost Chances

It wasn't so much the conversation with Stephen and Luke, or her guilt over what she didn't tell them about the red-haired mystery guy working in Standish Village. Nor was it even a result of digging through the pile of semi-packed belongings in the laundry room looking for Luke's missing lacrosse uniform that made Emma think of that letter from Skip. Not the one this past Christmas telling her Standish Village was for sale, but another one she did not remember seeing for some time, despite all her recent cleaning out and sorting in preparation for their upcoming move.

After Luke left for his game the next day, Emma couldn't stop thinking about the idea of "destiny" and "lost chances" and why it had suddenly occurred to her last night standing at the kitchen sink. Was it purely an analysis of her current motives? Or something else entirely? Something that perhaps originated from a long ago communication from her childhood pen pal. If only she could find that other letter! It wasn't like Emma to get rid of meaningful communication... on the other hand, it was very much like her to lose it.

It was close to two years after that trip to Florida that it came in the mail, to her father's house actually, reminding Emma again how long it had taken her to start her own life. She had been hesitant to open it, truthfully, since she had only recently managed to put the neglect of her friend out of her mind. But curiosity got the better of her, especially since the envelope was postmarked "Chatham, Massachusetts."

Okay, it had to be around here somewhere.

The letter had come right when she was moving the rest of her belongings to her new place, the first home of their own that she and her son had ever had. There wasn't all that much to move, as she recalled (thank god the place she was renting was at least partially furnished). But her desk, the one she'd had since she was a kid, was the one piece of furniture in her father's house she couldn't bear to leave behind. It was old and worn, and the drawers always stuck, but it was sitting here that she had written every letter to her childhood pen pal since the first summer they met, and also where she'd read every one she received, before stuffing them in one of the drawers, something she usually did even before writing her answer, many times forgetting all about them afterwards; the desk that was in Luke's bedroom right now.

Of course, she'd given it to Luke when he turned 12, and complained about having to do his homework at the kitchen table. After all, she didn't really use it anymore at that point, and remembered actually feeling happy that she could pass this one sentimental item down to her son. She'd cleaned out the drawers, of course, and even tried sanding the edges a little so they wouldn't stick as much; an effort that appeared to have been futile when Luke kept finding remnants of Emma's past crammed behind them. Like...like what? Then, she remembered. Like that picture. The one of her and Skip standing in front of Cottage #9 in Standish Village! The one he brought to her that afternoon last year and asked about.

Shoving the moving box she was in the midst of packing into the corner of the laundry room, Emma rushed down the hall to Luke's room and sat down in front of what three years before had become his desk. She smacked her hand firmly against the bottom drawer, the one that always stuck, and abruptly the drawer popped opened. Pushing aside a collection of Luke's old term papers, assorted index cards and a number of random paper clips and dried up highlighters, Emma reached to the very back of the drawer and felt around. Sure enough, trapped between its back edge and the bottom of the one above it, she could feel the corner of what seemed to be a tattered envelope.

Tugging roughly on the drawer, she managed at last to release it from the desk itself, the force of which effort managed to hurl both her and the drawer backward onto the rug. Emma struggled to a kneeling position, rubbed a sore elbow, then crawled back to the front of the desk and peered into the now vacated area that had once held the bottom drawer. On the rug, towards the back of the desk, rather than the expected envelope, lay a wad of torn paper, the condition no doubt a result of being trapped for years.

Discouraged by what felt like a failure of effort, Emma grabbed the find and tossed it into the trash, then contemplated the process of reinserting the drawer in the desk. As she stood and picked it up, however, another paper object, apparently still stuck to the bottom, suddenly fluttered to the floor.

Even before Emma picked it up, she recognized the faded handwriting scrawled its surface.

"Hi Emma!" (Skip's letter began cheerfully, which, in itself, seemed odd to Emma, since by all rights, Skip should not have even been speaking to her, much less cheerfully). *"Sorry it's been a while, but there's been a lot going on. And by the way, first I want to apologize for missing your call after that last time we were together."* (Missing my call? Emma thought? Did he not get that she never did call him that next morning in Florida?)

"I really intended for us to meet for lunch or something before you left (Skip's letter continued) *after Stephen threw us together on the beach. A little awkward, right? But it was really fine with me when he called again with his "detailed directions" ...and with Allison too...we both wanted you two to finally meet after all this time, and she would have adored Luke! And I really did want to have a good talk together, you know, like in the old days...on that old Cape Cod. It seemed like that might have been good for both of us right about then. But maybe it wasn't meant to be...destiny and all that. Anyhow, I digress... remember when we always tried to put that in all our letters when we didn't even get what it meant?"* (Emma smiled. Of course, she remembered, it was her favorite sixth grade vocabulary word.)

"So...when I got back from the beach that day (Skip wrote next), *Allison told me my Mom called and that Dad had a heart attack, so naturally we forgot about everything else and just jumped on the first plane to New Jersey. I bet we were already in the air by the time you called, that's how fast it all happened. I'm so sorry...I felt bad when I remembered about our plans later, but then one thing led to another... you know how it goes...and all of sudden so much time went by that I, well, I just felt like an idiot writing to you after so long."*

Then there was a space after which several lines had been crossed out. Eventually the letter continued, though in a different color ink, apparently written some time later (after he found a new pen, Emma guessed, because that would be just like...just like...me! The realization startled her and for a few moments, she sat silently, simply holding the letter in her hand. Then she looked down and began to read again.

"*So I guess I'm writing now because I thought of you today* (Skip's letter went on). *Okay, it's not like I don't think of you a lot of days, but what I mean is that I'm sitting here in the apartment in the carriage house behind my parents' summer place and playing old records, and yeah, you're right, I've got that stupid old Patti Page song playing again. I just don't know what it is about this old dumb song, but it makes me think about a lot of things in my life...like what I could have done differently, and what maybe I wish I had done instead of what I did...I don't know, I guess this all sounds kind of crazy, huh?*"

Actually, no, not to Emma it didn't, because it was a place she had been many times, so, why wouldn't Skip...I mean why wasn't it just natural that they would be in the same place again...together...like they always were.

"*If you're wondering what I'm doing on the Cape, Emma* (the letter continued), *I guess I should confess that I'm not really sure myself why I'm here. Of course, I went home to be with my Mom when Dad got sick, and then after he died, I stayed in New Jersey to help out with, you know, everything. But then after a couple weeks, when I was supposed to go home to Florida, well, I somehow just ended up here instead. Allison has tried to be understanding, and even came up here a few times, but I think she might be giving up on me, kind of like my whole family is. They want to sell this place, and I don't...but I don't really know what I want.*

I've been working back at the boatyard again, and spending a lot of time just cruising around Pleasant Bay, hoping I'll figure out what it is I want from life. Did I have some destiny other than the one I chose? And have I lost whatever chance I might have had to fulfill it? I wish you were here to help me decide. I wish we were kids again, back at Standish Village. I feel like then I'd know exactly what to do."

At this point, the letter abruptly ended with a quickly scrawled "*Love, Skip.*" And now, as she held it in her hand, it occurred to her that she may never have answered it. Or did she? Why wouldn't she have answered this communication, unless she was a truly terrible person? Here was her good friend clearly in trouble…no, not just a good friend, but possibly her best friend in the world…the one who not only knew and understood her better than anyone else, but also the one for whom, perhaps, the reverse was true.

All these years later, though, no matter what she may or may not have done in the past, she suddenly knew that somehow, she needed to answer this letter right away. The question was, where was Skip now and how could she go about finding him?

Chapter Twenty-Five: Turning Point (2003)

Despite her best intentions, it wasn't until the first weekend in May that Emma went back to Standish Village, and by then Stephen had committed to a buying trip for his antique business and was not able to come along...or so he claimed. Emma simply suspected his enthusiasm for ghost hunting had waned.

It wasn't as if Emma had neglected her responsibilities as the new owner of Standish Village...she had actually called Ted Parker several times in the interim, and he assured her that things were moving ahead on schedule. And Emma was also reassured by the consistent arrival of bills for building supplies, plumbing services, etc.; if writing large checks on a regular basis could be considered reassuring, that is.

It was, in fact, a bit frightening to watch her inheritance sliding slowly out of the bank, but Emma kept telling herself that it would ultimately result in Standish Village opening for a successful summer season, and thus restoring her tentative account balance. Another somewhat disturbing development, however, was that her landlord had indeed sold the house she and Luke were renting, and that currently all her worldly belongings were piled in a corner of Stephen and Jim's warehouse, while she and Luke were camped out at Joel and Missy's.

"It's no problem at all!" Missy had declared exuberantly when Emma apologized for appearing on their doorstep. "We have plenty of room! Stay as long as you need to."

Sitting on their guest room bed with a frilly pink pillow on her lap, Emma couldn't help but examine more closely what it was she truly needed. It seemed unlikely that, as the embroidered message on the pillow declared, "It is not the destination but the journey itself that matters;" especially since the journey might possibly be going in the wrong direction.

"Yeah, well, look at it from my perspective," Luke said, when she expressed her discouragement earlier that afternoon. "Try calling someone for a prom date when you're sitting on a lace canopied bed and a row of My Pretty Ponies are watching you from across the room."

Joel's youngest daughter had graciously moved in with her sister, so Luke could take over her room, which to Emma seemed like a generous offer at the time, but now she wasn't so sure.

"Maybe Lily will let you bring one of the ponies with you to the Cape this weekend," she teased, "you know, just so you feel more at home?"

"Very funny, Mom," Luke said, but smiled nonetheless, which was probably why, Emma realized later, she let her son miss a day of school on Friday so they could spend more time at Standish Village.

"What can they do, fire me?" Emma asked, when Luke expressed some concern over his mother taking the day off as well. She had already handed in her resignation, and while she had a nagging feeling it may not have been the perfect idea to "burn her bridges," as Stephen would say, it was somewhat liberating, nonetheless. So much so, that Emma found herself stuffing the back of the Jeep with boxes of her personal belongings when she and Luke set out for the Cape early Friday morning.

"Just getting a jump on the move!" she remarked cheerfully, when she saw Luke eyeing her efforts skeptically.

"Probably a good plan," he remarked somewhat dubiously, then climbed in the passenger side and closed the door.

"So anyhow," Luke began, once they were on the road, "how exactly am I going to help you figure out if these people you keep talking about are really people, or...you know...um...not?"

"Do I, like, touch them and see if my hand goes through them, wave garlic at them...or something?" he went on.

"Don't be silly," Emma said. "If you see them and talk to them like I see them and talk to them, then they are just who they are...nice people helping out...regardless of your uncle's cynicism."

"Anyhow, garlic is for vampires, not ghosts," she added.

"Good to know," Luke said.

"Besides," Emma went on as she slowed at the exit to the Sagamore Bridge, "apparently I might have been overreacting."

"What do you mean?" Luke asked.

"Well, last week I wrote checks to Charlie and Alice for some of the supplies they bought...and also Ted to pay some roofing guy...and...well...all the checks were cashed," she explained.

"And you're saying ghosts don't cash checks," Luke said.

"It's unlikely they would," Emma replied sheepishly. "And I doubt they have bank accounts either."

"I guess maybe I just got caught up in the whole mysterious way this all came about," she admitted, as they crossed the bridge onto the Cape. "You know, like how I found out about Standish Village being for sale, and then felt like I was compelled to buy it; like I couldn't help myself, you know, even though it wasn't the most practical thing to be doing."

Luke was silent.

"Maybe I just wanted to have an excuse for doing what I really wanted to do in the first place," Emma said, the finality in her voice surprising even her.

Luke still didn't respond.

"What's wrong?" Emma asked.

"What do you mean?" Luke said.

"I mean, how come you're not saying anything?" Emma replied. "I just admitted that maybe I did the wrong thing buying this place, and even made up some crazy thing in my head about ghosts urging me to do this, and even helping me, so I wouldn't back out, and you're just sitting there like it's all fine and good."

"At the very least, I expected an 'I told you so'," she added.

Luke turned to look at his mother, and grinned.

"I'm just disappointed I'm not going to meet any ghosts," he said. "But I guess I'll just have to live with that."

Emma laughed.

"Yeah, I guess you will," she said.

When they at last turned into the driveway of Standish Village and started driving down the hill toward the cottages, Emma felt unexpectedly relieved to see the small cluster of Adirondack chairs at the bottom of the stairs to Cottage #9. It was not like she hadn't told Ted Parker she and Luke were coming, but always before, this had been sort of a prelude to a conversation that went something like this:

"Coming?" Ted would respond, "Oh you mean you'll be coming out to the Cape?"

As always, Emma had the sneaking suspicion that the idea of anyone living anywhere else but Cape Cod was inherently unimaginable.

"Yes," Emma would explain, "you know, to see how things are going? To help out where I can?"

The latter inquiry would usually be followed by a silence, which Emma generally took to mean that Ted Parker, as well as the others working on her property, could not fathom how she could actually be of any "help."

Then Ted Parker would clear his throat hesitantly and say, "Well that's great! We'll see you then!"

Of course, Emma had not yet told him specifically when she would be arriving, but that didn't seem to matter, and besides, Ted Parker had already hung up before she came to this realization. Nonetheless, this time, as she drove into the property, everyone seemed as if they were waiting for her to arrive.

"Well, look at that!" Emma said to Luke, pointing to the occupants of the Adirondack chairs next to her cottage. "There they all are!"

Luke leaned forward in his seat and squinted through the windshield.

"Where?" he said. "I don't see anyone, just a bunch of chairs."

Emma slammed on the brakes halfway down the drive and turned to her son in horror.

"You don't see them?" she demanded. "All my new friends? Charlie? And Alice and Ted? Are you telling me that..."

Luke stared at her solemnly, then suddenly leaned back and burst into laughter.

"Of course, I do, Mom," he said, gasping for breath. "I was just teasing! You know...the whole ghost thing..."

"Very funny," Emma grumbled. "But you didn't fool me for a second. I knew what you were doing."

"Sure you did," Luke chuckled. "That's why you just peeled two years-worth of rubber off your tires."

Emma glared at him, then drove the rest of the way down the hill and pulled into the driveway next to the cottage, as her three friends waved cheerfully, and rose to greet them.

"So this is the blueberry pie man!" Alice declared, as Luke climbed out of the car.

"It certainly is," Luke said, glancing toward Cottage #9. "And I certainly hope there's one waiting inside."

Alice smiled.

"Of course, there is!" she exclaimed, as she possessively linked her arm through Luke's. "I made it fresh this afternoon."

"Charlie, Ted, Alice, this is my son, Luke," Emma said as the two men reached out and shook hands with Luke.

"Great to meet ya!' Charlie said, "I been hearin' a lot about ya. You're the photographer, right?"

"I guess," Luke said. "I mean I like taking pictures, but I don't know that I'm actually a ..."

"Oh bosh," Charlie declared, "none a' that nonsense! Lemme see what you got, and I'll decide!"

"Used to do quite a bit a' that myself, ya know," he added, clapping Luke on the shoulder. "Back in the old days, for the Cape Cod Times, and what's that other thing? Oh yeah, Life Magazine."

Life Magazine? Emma wondered. How could he have possibly ...but then looking at the grinning white-haired man, she found herself thinking, why not?

Ted Parker, meanwhile, was rambling on to Luke about "water properties" and Parker Realty's philosophy on land values, but Emma knew that Luke, his mind focused on pie, was only half listening. Meanwhile, she wasn't listening at all, but instead was looking around at the new and improved Standish Village.

Not only were the cottages bright and welcoming, with their fresh coats of paint and shiny new porch screens, but the paths between them were newly edged and lined with stones, and a clean, chunky layer of crushed shell covered the individual parking spots. The scrub pines appeared to have been lightly pruned as well, and in the distance, a row of freshly painted, red rowboats lined the shore of the tranquil pond. In fact, the whole property seemed more than ready to welcome summer visitors.

"Everything looks great!" Emma exclaimed, turning to the others. "But I imagine that means there's a pile of bills waiting in on my desk."

Ted Parker shrugged.

"There might be a few," he admitted sheepishly.

"Course these two here," he added, nodding in the direction of Charlie and Alice, "Wouldn't let me pay them hardly anything...and believe me, I tried."

"Well, I did let ya buy me lunch," Charlie said. "Besides, that other guy ya hired, Emma, what's his name? Frank? Peter? Philip? I forget…never was very good at names…but you know the one I mean… lives down the pond? Well, he's a helluva worker, anyhow. He probably did more around here than the rest a' us put together."

Ted Parker and Alice nodded enthusiastically.

"Yup," Ted Parker agreed. "It was almost like the guy owned the place himself. Every job always had to be just perfect before he considered it done."

"Well, sweetheart," Alice said, turning to Luke, "why don't we go inside and see about getting' you some a' that pie."

"Sound good to me!" Luke said. "You comin' Mom?"

"No, you go ahead," Emma said. "I need to take a little walk down the beach first."

"That beach?" Luke asked, pointing toward the little patch of sand lining the edge of White Pond. "Why?"

"I think I know where that guy lives," Emma said, "the guy Charlie's talking about. The one who did all the work around here?"

"Or at least where he's staying," she added.

 "I met his friend, Karen a while back," she explained. "We spent the evening together, in fact, and got to be pretty good friends over a couple bottles of wine. I'd hate for her to think I wasn't going to pay her friend, after all he did around here."

"She just lives right over there," Emma called over her shoulder, as she started down the hill toward the pond. "I'll be back soon."

"Okay," Luke said, "but don't expect me to save you any pie."

And with that, he followed the others up the steps to Cottage #9.

When Emma reached the house she thought belonged to Karen Davies, the pond had settled into its late afternoon stillness, and the sun was beginning to slip behind the pines on the opposite shore. The small cluster of dwellings at the other end of the beach seemed unusually quiet as she approached, but Emma attributed this to the season rather than an overall lack of residents. Still, however, as she climbed the front steps, she noticed that Karen's house appeared more than just temporarily vacated. The front porch was empty of the traditional Adirondack chairs and wobbly side tables, and intricate spider webs wound through the beams overhead.

Not seeing a bell, Emma knocked tentatively on the front door, which responded to her inquiry by creaking open on shaky hinges.

"Hello?" Emma called as she stepped cautiously into the house. "Karen?"

Her voice echoed through the empty front room.

"Ain't nobody home," came a voice from behind her.

Startled, Emma backed quickly out the door and turned around. Standing at the bottom of the porch steps was a stocky, gray-haired man dressed in waders and a flannel shirt. Over one shoulder he carried a fishing net and in his other hand he held a large metal bucket.

"What I mean to say is," the man went on cheerfully, "there ain't nobody home never. House has been empty for years."

Then he scratched his chin and slowly surveyed the structure from top to bottom.

"Damn shame, actually," he observed, "that no one bought the place a'fore it got in such bad shape."

"You ain't lookin' to do that, are ya?" he asked, somewhat eagerly it seemed to Emma.

"Um...no...no, I'm not," Emma said. "I was just...I mean, I thought..."

"I must have the wrong house," she added quickly, as she stepped off the porch to where the man stood. He grinned.

"Well then, maybe I can help youse find the right one," he remarked cheerfully.

"I'm looking for Karen Davies," Emma explained. "I'm pretty sure she told me that she and her son lived over here, but maybe I misunderstood."

The man scratched his chin again thoughtfully.

"Name don't ring a bell," he said at last.

"Me and my wife live over yonder," he added, gesturing towards the cluster of houses nearby. "Lived there practically 50 years, and we know most folks around here. 'Course there's some summer renters come and go."

Emma shook her head.

"I'm pretty sure she lives here year around," she told him. "Last time I saw her was just a few weeks ago, in fact."

"Well," the man replied, "I wish I could help ya. I can ask around if you'd like."

"No," Emma said. "That's okay. Like I said, I must have just misunderstood what she said...about where she and her little boy live, I mean."

"Suit yourself," the man said. "You have a nice day now, Miss."

Emma started to walk away, then suddenly stopped.

"By the way," she said. "Could I just ask you..."

The man turned to look at her once more.

"Did you...um...did you know the people who lived here before..." Emma began.

"The last owners, ya mean?" he inquired.

"Yeah, right," Emma said. "before they moved out and left it...left it empty."

"Not very well," the man said, then he grinned again and winked at her. "I know this might be hard to imagine, but truthfully, it was a bit before my time."

"Big family, they was," he remarked, gazing back at the house. "Used to come here summers, mostly. Had a bunch a' kids...or maybe they was a group a'cousins...I don't recall. My sister used to play with 'em, but they was mostly older than me, so they was pretty much all grown by the time I knew 'em.

"The parents kept the house for a while after that, and the family used to use it sometimes," he continued, "but then there was some sort of swimming accident one year, and after that, I don't think they come back."

"Swimming accident?" Emma asked cautiously.

"Yup," the man replied, rubbing his chin with the hand that still held the net. "Don't 'member much a' the details, but somethin' about a little boy that drowned...real tragic, regardless."

"I was away in the army then," he added, "and by the time I come back here to live, well...the house was already pretty much deserted."

Emma sighed.

"Okay, thanks," she said. "I guess I just have the wrong house."

"No problem," the man remarked, and adjusting the net on his shoulder, he turned and headed toward a cottage behind him, where a front porch light now gently glowed.

When Emma reached Cottage #9, the porch light here, as well as those on the row of cottages next to it, also shone softly in the fading daylight. Through the open kitchen window, Emma could hear Luke excitedly relaying the details of his most recent Lacrosse game, as a no doubt very patient Alice clattered about in the kitchen cupboards.

"And so then, the other team was so sure they won that the guy with the ball just dropped it on the ground," Luke was saying. "But in reality, there was a minute left and my friend, Zach, just scooped up the ball and tossed in our goal for the win!"

"Oh hey, Mom!" he said cheerfully, as Emma entered the kitchen, the screen door banging loudly behind her. "I was just telling Alice about the game. Cool, huh Alice?"

"Very cool," Alice said as she turned from the sink and winked at Emma. "Saved ya a piece 'a pie, girl. Ya interested?"

"Of course I am," Emma said, as she sank into a kitchen chair. "Bring it on."

"Did you find your friends, Mom?" Luke asked, peering expectantly around his mother, as if he feared someone else might be after the last piece of pie.

"Um no," Emma said. "No one was home."

Luke shrugged.

"Maybe tomorrow," he said.

"Right," Emma remarked, as she plunged her fork into the sugary blueness in front of her. "Maybe then I'll actually get to see them."

Chapter Twenty-Six: Allison (2003)

Two weeks later, Emma knelt in the sun-warmed soil of her garden in Standish Village. The perennials she'd planted over a month ago were now sprouting tender new leaves, and tiny flower buds perched uncertainly in the cautious greenery. Next to her on the ground sat a partially filled weed bucket, over which she had draped a still stiff pair of flowered gardening gloves, recently abandoned in favor of the feel of the damp earth on her fingers. As the sun began its daily descent toward the horizon, she dug affectionately around the new plantings with a newly purchased gardening claw.

It was still hard to believe that she'd given her last exam just a few days earlier (the pile of ungraded tests currently sitting on the kitchen table in Cottage #9), and that Luke was in Albany taking his final test today. Emma had promised him she'd be home on Saturday afternoon before he left for the prom, but just wanted to take one more quick trip to Standish Village, to make sure everything was ready for the Grand Opening on Memorial Day. As she yanked another invading weed free, Emma made a mental note to check on the corsage that Luke had supposedly ordered for his prom date.

"Emma?" A voice behind her inquired tentatively.

Emma turned and shielded her eyes, as she peered in the direction of the speaker silhouetted by the remaining sunlight. As she stood, wiping her hands on her jeans, her visitor came more clearly into view. She was a young woman about Emma's age, dressed in jeans and an oversized, faded blue oxford shirt, her blond hair pulled carelessly back with an orange scrunchie. The woman smiled.

"You're Emma, right?" she said, stepping into the garden. "

"Wow," she added, "this is going to be one gorgeous flowerbed in a few months. Did you plant it yourself?"

"I did!" Emma exclaimed proudly. "Well, actually, there was kind of a garden here before, but it was all overgrown, and well...I thought it would be really nice to restore it...for...for my new place."

Then Emma stood and observed the other woman curiously.

"I'm sorry," she said at last, "have we met? I mean you seem to know my name, and if someone in town introduced us...or something...I guess I'm feeling a little awkward that I've forgotten yours."

The woman turned her attention from the flowers back to Emma.

"Oh!" she said. "I'm so sorry. My fault entirely. No, we haven't met...I just heard you bought Standish Village and I came over to introduce myself. My parents have a place in Chatham and I was visiting them this weekend, so I thought maybe I'd just come by."

"I'm Allison," she added, extending her hand in Emma's direction. "Allison Murray."

"Oh...um..." Emma held her dirt-caked palms up in front of her, "...sorry. Nice to meet you."

Allison laughed.

"Oh yes, of course," she said, "we'll do the official handshake later."

"Sounds good," Emma said. "So...would you like a tour?"

"I'd love one," Allison said. "Just lead the way."

A while later, just when the daylight was beginning to fade, Emma and Allison climbed the steps of Cottage #9.

"How about a glass of wine?" Emma suggested.

"I thought you'd never ask," her guest replied.

"So, what made you decide to buy this place?" Allison asked, as she sat down at the kitchen table and carefully pushed the pile of ungraded exams to one side.

"Well," Emma explained, as she carried the bottle of wine and two glasses to the table and sat down herself, "I suppose partly those."

She pointed to the pile of papers and then proceeded to uncork the wine.

"I mean it's not that I don't like teaching, I do," she added. "But for a long time, I've just sort of felt like I was treading water, you know? Like I was always doing what everyone expected of me instead of...I don't know...This probably sounds stupid, but instead of fulfilling my true destiny."

"I guess I just got tired of lost chances," Emma went on, as she poured them each a glass of wine, "like I was letting my life pass me by without really reaching out and grabbing the opportunities that might be out there, and just, you know, letting them slip away instead."

Allison nodded.

"You sound just like my husband," she said and sighed. "He loved the Cape when he was a kid...and when he was older too. He said coming out here was what gave him real direction in his life, when nothing else seemed to. There was this crazy song he always used to play, something about "if you spend an evening you'll want to stay?"

"Watching the moonlight on Cape Cod Bay,'" Emma said and laughed. "And then you're sure to fall in love with that old Cape Cod.

Such a corny song, but you know, I kind of feel that way now, since I bought this place and fixed it up, I mean. I guess I never realized how important it was to me when I was a kid, but once I came here again, well, it brought back so many memories. I think, stupid as this sounds, I was happier back then than most other times in my life."

"Oh my god, yes!" Allison exclaimed. "My husband would so agree. If only he were still here, he would be so happy to see what you've done with Standish Village, to see it up and running again! For it to be like it was back when you were kids."

Emma studied her companion briefly.

"Wait," she said, "did you just say if he was still here? Is he..."

Allison hesitated and looked down at her glass of wine.

"You really don't know who I am, do you?" she remarked quietly.

Then she abruptly reached across the table and took Emma's hands in hers.

"Oh Emma," she said, "I'm so sorry, I thought you knew. He passed away eight years ago in that terrible fire...at his parents' house...in that little carriage house, you know? We were separated at the time, which...god...made it even more painful. It just took me so many years to get by all that...and...well, I guess I should have called you or something...but I thought for sure that someone...his parents or someone...I didn't mean for you to find out like this."

Allison's eyes filled with tears as she gazed helplessly at Emma.

"I thought..." she went on, "that, you know...you just weren't bringing it up because you didn't want to...I never thought you wouldn't realize who I was."

"But I guess that was kind of dumb of me, wasn't it?" she said, as she pulled her hands back and dropped them in her lap. "After all, we never actually met, but I always felt like I knew you so well, because my husband, he always talked about you and how all those years you were his best friend and everything…"

Emma stared back across the table as a silence fell between them.

"I'm just so, so sorry," Allison said at last.

"But…" Emma began hesitantly, "I thought you said your name was…".

"It's Allison," the young woman said, "Allison Murray."

Then she looked down at her lap again.

"But in 1995," she continued, "I was Allison Peterson."

"And Skip Peterson is…" Emma asked.

"Skip Peterson is…he was…my husband," Allison added softly.

Chapter Twenty-Seven: That Old Cape Cod (2018)

It was Emma's favorite time of day at Standish Village; one that varied with the seasons, of course, but was nonetheless always the same in terms of the slowly fading light and the gentle quiet that settled on the pond and the scrub pines, and eventually on the cottages themselves, from which the lights inside now began to softly glow. Even the geese seemed to realize it was time to settle in for the night, as their endless cacophony ceased and they slipped silently into the still waters of the waiting pond.

It was when the cooking smells from the separate dwellings mixed in the outside air, and the children's voices quieted, and became that one simple melody of childhood when dinner ends, and stories and baths and firm "good nights" take over the day. And it was when, for the last 15 years, Emma had taken her final walk through Standish Village, along the path that wound between the cottages, through the carpet of pine needles and among the scattered pine cones that no one ever felt the need to remove.

Often it did not seem that long ago to Emma that she cajoled a protesting, sticky, muddy Luke into a bath with the promise of his favorite story before bed...or for that matter, since she was that cranky pre-bedtime child herself, pleading for one more half hour outside while it was still light; when she was right here, in fact, at Standish Village...with her best friend, Skip. And now, she thought, as she walked down the last path to the beach, in a cottage on the hill behind her,

Luke was sudsing up a giggling little boy of his own; who gleefully splashed and shrieked through his bath, while his mom spent a few restful moments sipping her wine on the screened-in porch. Emma smiled as she wondered if they remembered to bring that roll of packing tape, just in case the screen needed repair.

The bench was still there after all these years, even though she doubted that either of her brothers remembered this long ago gift. Joel and Missy had stopped bringing the little girls to Standish Village in favor of trendier resorts, back when Ashley and Lily were in high school, and Stephen, after making it clear that cottages in the "mosquito-ridden woods" were "not his thing," had spent most of his visits staying down the road at the Chatham Bars. Recently, though, he and Jim had moved their antique business to Florida, which made their trips to the Cape fewer and far between.

But the bench her brothers had given her on the day of her Grand Opening 15 years ago was still as special to Emma as it was the first day she sat on it, and tonight, which was probably one of the last times she would do so, the feeling was no different. The Grand Opening had been difficult, of course, being that it took place just two weeks after Allison Murray came to Standish Village and told Emma about Skip's death.

Oh, clearly Allison hadn't intended it to be like that...a sudden moment of truth as the two women sat together in Cottage #9 sharing a bottle of wine, Emma thinking that Allison Murray was just a curious visitor to the Village and Allison assuming that Emma knew her actual identity. Not just who Allison was, but that her husband, Skip, Emma's best friend in the world, had died eight years earlier in the same fire that consumed the carriage house where Emma and her college friends once spent the summer. Still, in the hours and days that followed this revelation, Emma wandered the pathways of Standish Village in a grief-filled haze, planning the celebration of her potential future at the same time she mourned the loss of her past.

If I hadn't been for Luke and her brothers, and of course, Charlie and Alice and Ted, she might have given up on the whole thing. But the fact that they stood by her and encouraged her determination to move forward had made the eventual difference. That and another presence of which everyone else remained blissfully unaware, and one that Emma never mentioned to any of them in the weeks and years that followed.

She had her moments, naturally, when grief would overwhelm her daily responsibilities as the hands-on owner of the new Standish Village. But more and more regularly, whenever the memories and lost opportunities of the past would weigh her down, she would catch a glimpse of the young man with curly red hair disappearing around the back of one of the cottages. Or briefly see him trudging down the beach toward the cluster of houses where she once thought Karen lived, her new friend with whom she shared that one evening and then never heard from again.

Not only that, but every time Emma threw a wrench across the room in frustration, when a leaking pipe would just not stop dripping water no matter what she did, a sense of calm would abruptly come over her, and suddenly she would be able to easily resolve the plumbing issue. And also, there were all the nights Emma would go to bed stressing about how to accomplish a difficult task the next day, and by the time she was up the next morning ready to take it on, she'd find it finished, painted, fixed, or whatever was needed, already done.

Of course, she blamed these miraculous occasions on Charlie, despite his consistent denial, or even Luke, but after Charlie was gone (and Alice as well), and Luke off living a life of his own, the odd situation continued. Then after a while, she just got used to it, and as a result, a new self-confidence emerged, as well as strength she never imagined she could have. She was still the same old Emma, as she had often told Skip, but perhaps also the more capable one that had been inside her all the time.

She ran her hand across the engraved plaque on the back of the bench, worn and faded now from years of Cape Cod sun and storms. "In Memory of My Forever Best Friend, Skip, and Our Old Cape Cod," the plague read. Then she sank down on the splintery seat and gazed out at the pond.

The decision to sell Standish Village was not one that came about casually, of course…she'd been thinking about it for over a year, well before she mentioned it to either Luke or her brothers. But now that she had actually done it, it seemed somehow abrupt; as if she'd done so hastily, during a weak moment when the late nights and busy seasons full of broken plumbing and rotting porch steps, and endless tears in the screens had left her exhausted and disillusioned, with only a vague memory of her once optimistic attitude.

Just that morning, however, she had sat at her white dressing table, now somewhat rickety and fragile, and saw in the mirror not the ambitious thirty-eight year-old single mother yearning to finally take something from life, but a tired fifty-plus grandmother who had taken everything she could, and yes, loved every minute of it.

So now, maybe it was time to go, while "the going was good," as her father always used to say, when they packed the old station wagon at the end of their annual vacation at Standish Village and headed for home. Emma smiled as the memory returned of those last few childhood hours here; of making sure she'd packed all her clothes and books, and tiny treasured beach finds she would take home and carefully position on her bookshelves to remind of her another perfect summer.

Then, before squeezing in the backseat between her two brothers, she would quickly run next door to where Skip was sitting on the steps of his cottage...pretending not to care that Emma and her family were about to drive away...just sort of casually leafing through a comic book or rolling a yoyo up and down on its string.

"Oh," he'd say, trying to act surprised, "hi Emma, what's up?"

And instead of falling for his stupid act or getting all mad that he didn't even acknowledge she was leaving, and it would be another whole year until they were together again, she would just grin and answer, "the sky, the clouds, the birds, the national debt..." just like always. Then they would both start laughing...as always. Then Skip would say, "I guess I'll see ya when I see ya," and Emma would answer, "Not if I see you first." And as Emma turned to run back to her car, they'd both call out, "don't forget to write!"

And the funny thing was, at least funny for kids their age, that they did write; letter after letter, sharing everything about their lives, their thoughts, their feelings, back when there was no such thing as email or Snapchat or even Facebook to keep them connected. But what had really kept them connected, Emma thought, as she leaned back on the bench was right here, not just here on "that old Cape Cod," but here in Standish Village, where some part of her, some part of both of them, would always exist, even when neither of them were any longer here.

"So, you're thinking about that again, are you?" he said, as he sat down beside her and flung his arm across the back of the bench. Even in the fading daylight his red curly hair and goofy lopsided grin stood out against the silent backdrop of the now sleepy village, and as always, still made her smile.

"Thinking about what again?" Emma demanded petulantly.

"You know," he told her, shoving her playfully with his other arm. "The whole 'am I making a big mistake by selling this place' and 'what am I thinking giving up the only thing that ever made me really happy?' stuff."

"Because it's not, you know," he added.

"Not what?" Emma asked hesitantly.

"The only thing that ever made you happy," he replied.

Emma said nothing, but simply continued to stare out at the pond. The last rays of sun slipped behind the trees on the opposite shore, and somewhere beyond the raft, a single fish jumped, gently disrupting the surface of the water with a few lazy rippling circles.

"There's Luke, for example," he went on. "You can't tell me that even the fact of his very existence hasn't brought you joy all these years, not to mention what an awesome kid he's always been."

"And there's Joel and Missy and the girls, and Stephen and Jim," he said. "Not everyone has all those people to love them, laugh with them, or care about what happens to them."

Emma shrugged.

"Okay," she said. "You win...again."

"But you should have told me," she insisted. "Or someone should have told me! Instead of letting me go on believing that you were still out there somewhere. Tell me that I didn't have us anymore, and there would never be an us to make me happy again."

He sighed and leaned forward, his elbows on his knees.

"And what would you have done differently," he said, "if you knew, I mean. Would your life really have been all that different?"

"Of course, it would have!" Emma exclaimed.

"How?" he asked, turning to her with a smile.

"Well, maybe I wouldn't have..." Emma began, and then stopped.

"Wouldn't have what, Emma?" he said gently. "Wouldn't have done all the things that were your choice to do in the first place?"

"You're a lot of things, Emma Lakin," he added, "but indecisive isn't one of them."

"Well that's not what you used to say," Emma declared, folding her arms across her chest defiantly. "You used to tell me that I just let life happen to me...that I didn't move forward unless someone pushed me."

He looked over at her and sighed. Then he turned his head slowly, and silently took in their surroundings. Emma cautiously followed his gaze.

"What about all this?" he said. "What about Standish Village and the last 15 years you made this your life? And, I might add, very successfully so."

"Oh, like you had nothing to do with this," Emma said. "Like you weren't the one who pushed me into this, who helped me create it...who made sure I met Charlie and Alice, and even Ted."

"Plus," she added, "how was it that every time I thought I couldn't fix something I magically figured out how to do it, and every time I was totally stressed about all the work that needed to be done around here, half of it was magically taken care of?"

"But Emma," he said quietly, "I haven't been here since 1995. How could I have done all that?"

Then he stood, stuck his hands in his pockets, and smiled down at her.

"You did it all by yourself," he said, "just like I always knew you could...and like you always knew you could, too...and I'm proud of you for it."

Emma stood as well.

"Does this mean you're leaving?" she asked, "I mean, leaving for good?"

He nodded.

"Yup," he said, "what I came to do is done."

"But I'm not sure...I mean I don't think I can..." Emma protested.

"Not without you..." she added hopelessly.

But he just slowly turned, and shaking his head sadly, began to walk down the beach. That was when Emma saw them, the woman and the boy standing at the end of the sand, watching silently as Skip approached them.

"Karen?" Emma called, surprised to suddenly see the friend who had abruptly disappeared from her life. "Will? What...I mean where have you...why didn't you...."

By then Skip had reached the pair and when Karen held out her hand, he took it in his and turned to face Emma once more.

"But I can't..." she began, "I mean can't you stay? It's that old Cape Cod, remember? Skip? Don't you remember?"

But he didn't answer. He just lifted his free hand and waved sadly, and as the daylight at last faded away, the three figures disappeared silently into the night.

"I'll see ya when I see ya," Emma said to the empty beach, but as the moon rose slowly over the pond, she knew she never would see him again.

About the Author

Erni Johnson was a literature and writing teacher, newspaper reporter and feature editor, public relations specialist, and innkeeper at various times in her life. She and her artist husband, Daryl, have now followed the sound of the waves to their beloved Cape Cod. In addition to this novel, she has written seven others, as well as a collection of short stories, and a cookbook filled with recipes and anecdotes from the Johnsons' innkeeping days.

More information on Erni Johnson's work can be found at: https://www.amazon.com/Erni-Johnson/e/B07CHXFRN6

Erni also welcomes feedback at: ernijohnson16@gmail.com

Printed in Great Britain
by Amazon